CLUSTER LUCK

THE ALICE LUCK SPACE ADVENTURES
BOOK 2

H. CLAIRE TAYLOR

ISBN: 978-1-959041-03-0 (H. Claire Taylor)

FFS Media, LLC

www.ffs.media

contact@hclairetaylor.com

PROLOGUE

Say goodbye to Blerg VFP69 as we rejoin the Lexicographers for yet another breakthrough on the name of God. It takes us longer to reach them than it did before, since the universe has expanded significantly in the meantime.

Since the last time we attended the symposium, both Dale and Hammy have died (to the great pleasure of their wives and ex-wives, who were well and truly sick of hearing theories about what letter might follow H in the mysterious name of the thing that's in charge of everything and nothing).

Both deaths were unnatural.

Dale's resulted from his obsession with why the letter H in the Roman alphabet of Blerg VFP69 would be the thing of all things to start the name of God. Lost in his head one day, he failed to watch where he was slithering and fell right into the gaping maw of something known on his planet as a pip.

To visualize a pip, imagine a rattlesnake turned inside out, covered in parasites, and absolutely gushing with mucus. Then imagine it a thousand times bigger than a rattlesnake and hiding in a burrow with its jaws open, inside-out lips even with the ground. The reason more of Dale's kind didn't die by pip was because the beasts were incredibly easy to spot and didn't move especially fast. In fact, they rarely moved at all. Dale slithered straight down the pip's gullet, and in a lot of ways, he deserved it. At least, his ex-wife thought so.

Hammy's death earned him slightly more sympathy from those who knew him. His wife murdered him.

The three Lexicographers who discovered the second letter knew neither Dale's nor Hammy's name, though, I should remind you, we don't either. Dale and Hammy are just placeholder names for these truly forgettable beings in the universe who proved themselves letter-smart but ultimately too stupid to live.

These three new upstarts called a meeting of the Lexicographers, and because the previous announcement had included a light projector, this one included a holographic projection. It didn't need to. Letters are two-dimensional. They don't need to be viewed in three dimensions, and it's generally best if they're not.

But flair was flair.

The holographic projector was on the fritz. One of the presenters kicked it once then kicked it again with his other foot. Then he slapped it around a bit with one of his meaty tentacles. It stopped sputtering and produced a clear image. But not of a letter.

"Oh no!" The second presenter rushed forward and hurriedly flipped the off switch on the projector. He'd forgotten to remove the graphic image he was gazing at the night before and replace it with the second letter! What had been projected in midair for the gallery to see was the final stages of a binary star pair in a death spiral, just before collision. Very private viewing, and offensive to many.

"This is off to a great start," muttered the third presenter, who we might as well call Vince. Vince had no ground to stand on for sarcastic remarks, since he'd mostly hitched his wagon to the other two, who were vastly more intelligent beings than he but not intelligent enough to realize it, so dazzled were they by his impressive string of failed marriages.

Once the pornographic stars were removed, the first presenter, who I think we should call Garbob, though I can't explain that inclination, called the assembly to order.

The brief flash of the sexy binary stars had elicited strong stomach acidity from all the loose esophagi in the room, and it was $T=2$ (unit not established) before the resulting belching quieted enough for those at the center of the semicircular arena to be heard.

Garbob took the lead, since Jimjam was humiliated into silence by the hologram incident and Vince was only there to look good.

"We have discovered another letter of the name of the thing that is behind everything and nothing. We have performed exhaustive calculations ..." As he said it, it dawned on him that only he and Jimjam had done any calculations at all, while Vince had been all but useless. "We have factored in the first letter of the name, and we have conclusively discovered the second. We have good reason to suspect it is in the same language as the first, and you will soon understand why."

"Roman," said Vince. "We believe it is in the Roman alphabet."

Normally any mention of a language from a bastard planet like Blerg VFP69 would make an orthodox intergalactic assembly like the Lexicographers burp and grunt their disapproval, but ever since the initial discovery, they had resigned themselves to the fact that, while simple, the first letter matched no other alphabet but the Roman, and that the letter was a strange one, a letter that seemed to have no true reason to exist, since it was often silent anyway: H.

Garbob continued: "We will now reveal the second letter of the name of the everything and nothing, the great contradiction, the reasons our wives have left us." He nodded to Jimjam, who was hoping to redeem himself after the humiliation. Jimjam turned on the projector again, and this time there was not an erotic astronomical event hovering above the surface, but a great big letter. It floated in all its unnecessary 3D glory for the room to see. The presenters held their breath, bracing for the praise.

"I think there's been some mistake," came a deep voice from the crowd. "We already discovered that one."

Garbob had suspected this might happen. "As I said before, we have taken the first letter into account in our calculations for the second. The second letter is the same as the first."

"What a steaming sack of shit," said another voice from the benches. "HH? There's no word that starts with HH!"

"The name of everything and nothing does, *Kenneth*," Garbob shot back. "The name of the reason my wife left me does! It begins with HH!"

"I demand you show me your calculations!" hollered a blobby thing.

"I'll show you *this!*" Vince shouted, grabbing a fistful of his robe and genitals and shaking them at the heckler. "I got a whole cluster here I'm happy to show you, you old space suck!"

As you can imagine, the scene devolved quickly from there with the Lexicographers shouting and comparing genital size, which was really no competition at all, considering there were a few species in the mix who were more than ninety percent genitals in their physical makeup.

After fists and tentacles and bone nubs and flippers and spiny appendages started flying, two of the geriatric Lexicographers didn't survive to make it home to their wives that evening.

And amidst the grappling and acidic slime squirting, the second letter of the name of God rotated silently in holographic form:

H

CHAPTER
ONE

Captain Alice Luck was chugging her eighth glass of water for the day when DeepCUT *Emergence* touched down in the hidden hanger of the Depot headquarters. Not even the booster she'd requested in her cabin had put a dent in the hangover from a week of partying on a faraway resort planet. Jaspariampt had proven an ideal place to unwind after the questionably successful trial mission. It was a land of buffets, and she was fairly sure she'd eaten a little bit of everything on offer and a *lot* of a few things. The bite-size morsels that tasted like shrimp in cocktail sauce and emitted a strange sound like a giggle when you bit their heads off were her favorite. She must've eaten a thousand of them, and would've had more if she hadn't split her time with ingesting shots of distilled alcohol and letting Dan Zone from the Ministry of Weapons and Culture introduce her to the planet's many water sports.

But now it was back down to Earth. Literally.

The ship jolted upon touchdown, and the last of Alice's water sloshed out of the glass and got her between the eyes.

"You all right, Captain?" Susy Machiavelli asked from the chair beside the captain on the ship's bridge.

It wasn't the first time, nor would it be the last, that Vel wondered how Liz Windsor and the higher-ups at the Depot had decided that Alice Luck, this naïve Texan with no discernible leadership qualities, was the best for the job. While Alice showed an occasional flash of brilliance, the position should've gone to Vel, and everyone knew it. Everyone except those making the hiring decisions, that was.

"Yeah, I'm good," Alice said, squinting against the pulsating pain in her temples. "Felt refreshing, actually."

"I'm not talking about the water. I'm talking about the hangover you keep pretending you don't have."

"I'm not pretending. I feel great."

"You threw up just before we entered Earth's atmosphere."

"So? People throw up. It doesn't have to mean anything."

"It does mean something," Vel said. "It's called a *symptom*."

"Okay, fine. I'm a little dehydrated. Trust me, I've had way worse. You should've seen me after my twenty-first birthday. Hangover lasted for two full days. I didn't rise from bed until the morning of the third day. Friends called me Drunk Jesus for months after."

The grinning, unwrinkled face of their Depot liaison, Liz Windsor, popped on the large screen in front of them. "WELCOME BACK!"

Alice grimaced and clutched at her head. "Allura! Volume down!"

"Yes, Daddy," replied the silky-smooth voice of the ship's operating system.

"I hope your vacation to Jaspariampt was restful and rejuvenating," Liz Windsor said, her grin never wavering. "We already have your next client lined up. Please disembark from your ship when you're ready, and I will brief you on the mission and make the introduction." Her face disappeared promptly, leaving only the gentle buzz from the ship's ventilation system behind.

"Wow," Caid Sonorian said from his seat at the kitchenette in the back of the bridge, "that's a harsh transition."

The organic hologram had enjoyed the vacation, but since he always lived in the moment, it didn't especially move the dial for his quality of life one way or another. He was as present as ever, and while he couldn't experience many of the sensory delights, owing to his having no mass, he had felt a sort of pride for the crew and their ability to let go, especially Dan. The minister from Pangoliarch had dropped his armor as much as an armored being could.

Vel, on the other hand, hadn't let her guard down like Caid would've liked to see. In fact, the lieutenant of DeepService Team One had been as guarded as he'd ever seen her. No matter how many times he'd suggested a counseling session to discuss her feelings on having been captured and held prisoner by the Alliance rebels, she wouldn't let him in. And they had been making so much progress prior to the capture! She'd even opened up about her father!

"Harsh transition?" said Vel. "It's not like we didn't just have a week to muck around and act foolishly." She breezed past Alice, who had reached toward her for a helping hand out of her chair.

Dan hurried over and helped his captain stand, and she

thanked him with a nod. "You're not, you know, dehydrated?" she asked.

"Hungover, you mean?" Dan asked. "No. My cells retain water much more efficiently than a human's. Here." He reached in his jumpsuit pocket then handed her a small packet. "I don't need my first booster today. Liz Windsor will have coffee."

"Dan, you goddamned saint." Alice swallowed it down. "You think I could get my second allotted for the day without Allura catching on?"

Dan looked her over, a cringe revealing his grim prognosis. "Might be worth a try."

And so she tried, and succeeded, and Dan was right. After her third booster of the day—one more than anyone was supposed to have—Alice Luck was starting to feel herself again, enough so that her thoughts became consumed almost entirely by notions of pizza and cheeseburgers.

Oh yeah, she could *definitely* house a few of those now that she was back on her home planet.

The crew filed off the ship, Vel in the lead, followed closely by Dan and Caid, then finally the captain, taking up the rear and remembering that there were a few delicious places to grab food nearby. The Depot headquarters was, after all, located in Austin, Texas, where she'd lived prior to accepting this job. Disguised as an office supply store, the headquarters was conveniently positioned a few minutes' drive south of downtown. Alice could pop out, order some tacos, a plate of brisket, and a meat-stacked pizza and be back within the hour, assuming she could slip away from all this mission and client nonsense.

Liz Windsor clapped her hands excitedly as the crew exited the ship through the hangar deck port. The liaison stood all alone, dressed in a formfitting knee-length red dress, her hair pinned back and slightly coiffed on top. Alice wondered if the woman had been taking style tips from the local TV weather woman.

"Where's Mike?" Dan asked.

For a split second, Liz Windsor's grin faltered. "Oh, he's no longer with us. The Depot required someone be held accountable for the blackout that we experienced at the end of your trial mission, and I'm afraid that, upon my close investigation, Mike was completely responsible for it. He's been decommissioned."

"That doesn't sound good," Alice muttered, checking with Dan. He shook his head to confirm that it was not good.

"Before I introduce you to your next client, we have a bit of, shall I say, *housekeeping*."

"You shall," Alice said absent-mindedly as she experienced a phantom whiff of meaty, cheesy, oniony goodness. Her mouth watered. If she didn't get some good eats soon, she would become a problem. Hangry had never been her best look, and she had come to peace with the fact.

"Follow me, then." Liz Windsor tip-tapped across the concrete floor, but not toward the rest of the building. Instead, she led them over to a second, slightly roomier ship whose exterior appeared noticeably more polished than that of the *Emergence*. "This is the *Constant*, your new, permanent ship. Now that you're no longer in your trial period, the Depot is comfortably upgrading you to more expensive machinery."

Vel stared at the craft, inhaling deeply and feeling something tight let go between her shoulder blades. She was so used to holding her breath that she almost never noticed it until whatever threat or annoyance was causing the tension ceased to exist.

DeepCUT *Emergence* had held up, and it had even saved their asses on Bacc'nalia when the Alliance or whoever had tried to snipe them from the rooftops, but the model held no prestige. It was a Cosmic Utility Transit, not the kind of battleship they would need were they to take on the rebels again.

Vel's mind drifted back to her time in captivity, and the things that had been said, the things she'd learned …

"Oh hell no." Alice chopped the air with her hands to cut through the new nonsense, snapping Vel's attention back to the present moment. "No, no, no. Sorry, Liz Windsor, but absolutely not. I don't know who Fillitine 8700 is, but he sounds like a real prick."

Vel couldn't believe their good luck. "Hold on. *Constant* is equipped with a Fillitine 8700 operating system?" This was better than she'd hoped.

Liz Windsor was clearly taking pleasure in being able to offer a top-of-the-line system to the crew, as her usual plastic grin was now more of a self-assured smirk.

"No," Alice said again. "Allura 4000 is part of the crew."

"That is untrue," Liz Windsor said. "She is a piece of software."

But Alice would not be deterred. "Well, who isn't? She's as much a part of our crew as my bodiless boy Caid, and I won't be going on another mission without her."

Vel was half prepared to see their captain lose her job on the spot, but instead, Liz Windsor blinked rapidly then said, "I understand. Unfortunately, Allura 4000 is incompatible with the operating system of *Constant*. If you want to keep Allura, you'll need to continue your work on *Emergence*."

"Deal!"

Vel grunted. "I'm sure you can program Fillitine 8700 to call you Daddy, Captain."

Alice curled her upper lip. "Not the same. What Allura and I have is special, built on a foundation of trust."

"You had her start calling you that on day one. I promise," Vel continued, "if it's the last thing I do, I'll find a way to program it to call you whatever you want. Just let us take the *Constant*."

Alice appeared to consider it, but Vel knew there was never any telling what was going on behind those blue eyes. The captain strolled closer to *Constant*. "What's so special about this ship, anyway? It looks exactly like—" She bounced backward and barely kept her feet under her.

"Oops! Sorry!" said Liz Windsor. "Forgot to disarm the force field."

"Force field?" Alice muttered, staring at the ship with something not unlike reverence, and for a brief and shining moment it seemed like she'd changed her mind.

She turned to the rest of the crew, crinkling her nose like a rabbit. "Any ship that requires a force field must be pretty weak. Y'all saw how *Emergence* took that fire back on Bacc'nalia. Like a goddamn *champ!*"

Vel glanced at Dan, who, to her horror, seemed to agree with the sentiment. The man lived his life covered in blaster-resistant armor, so of *course* he didn't see the benefit of a force field.

The lieutenant narrowed her eyes at the minister of weapons and culture. Alice had clearly gotten to him on their vacation. He might even be in love with the captain. He seemed the puppy-dog type.

It wasn't that Alice Luck didn't have a certain charm to her. Vel could appreciate that well enough. And her captain *had* come to her rescue when she was captured, despite it being the very worst decision. Vel could trust her for that much. What she couldn't trust her for was to pick the strategically smart thing over the fun thing.

That tiny defect would undoubtedly be the death of them all.

It could be manipulated easily enough, though. Once Vel had someone figured out so precisely, she could get them to do or believe whatever she needed them to. If only Vel knew where exactly she came down on this whole Depot mess, which side had the stronger point ...

"We'll get *Emergence* cleaned and reset for you, then," Liz Windsor said, failing to mention who comprised that "we," now that Mike was decommissioned. "In the meantime, why don't you follow me inside and I'll brief you on your next assignment before you meet the client?"

As DeepService Team One followed the woman across the hangar, Alice cast a quick look over her shoulder at *Emergence*, knowing Allura 4000 was waiting there for them.

Yes, the operating system called her Daddy, and yes, she enjoyed it more than she had any right to, but that wasn't where the system's appeal ended. No, Alice was fairly certain that Allura had another useful kink built in, the one that had tripped the power grid all the way back at HQ to buy them time, and one that might someday save their asses again.

Allura liked to be *bad*.

CHAPTER
TWO

Alice sipped her freshly brewed coffee, wishing she had a fat cheeseburger to go with it but also grateful as the caffeine took the edge off her hangover. The crew sat on couches ringed around a table with a holographic projector that gave off a lazy glow until Liz Windsor pulled up the schematics of the next assignment.

To Alice, the image looked like a typical and unremarkable spattering of stars hovering in midair. It was unimpressive and generic.

Woohoo, she thought without real enthusiasm. *More stars. Yippee.*

The rest of the crew, however, did not appear to feel the same. After a moment of recognition, then shock, came the uproar.

"You gotta be kidding me," Vel muttered.

"No! Liz Windsor!" Dan declared. "Tell me this isn't what I think it is!"

Even Caid furrowed his brow, adding, "This is a lot to unpack."

"What?" Alice demanded. "What am I missing?" She looked from Dan to Vel to Caid, but none answered her.

Liz Windsor soldiered on. "This is Star Cluster B, located in the Iota-Pi sector of our universe. The planet that has elicited the help of the Depot is called known locally as Trauna. Our client is—"

"A complete void-brained space nut," Dan muttered through hands clutching his face.

Liz Windsor perked up. "Mr. Zone, I'm shocked to hear you take that tone. You're supposed to be our cultural liaison."

"Exactly. That's why I know this is doomed to fail. There's no diplomacy with people who won't play by any rules. What's the official name of Trauna, Liz Windsor?"

The liaison's grin tightened but held on by a thread. Then, her tone evenly cold, she said, "Hopper TAP389, which is not to say—"

Vel and Dan locked wide eyes and shouted, "TAP!"

Alice was, of course, completely lost. "What's a TAP?"

"Totally Awful Planet," Dan replied.

"Whoa, whoa, whoa …" Alice held up both palms. "That doesn't sound great, but I am *so* lost. What's happening here? Back up and explain it to me like I'm stupid."

"There's nothing to explain," Liz Windsor said. "I think our client is quite lovely, having spent a little time with him. Star Cluster B has a nasty reputation, sure, but it's unwise to trust stereotypes. You can miss out on a lot of lovely individuals that way. That being said, we understand this mission has some unique challenges, so you'll be given a full seventy-two hours of ship time to complete it."

"How'd he even get outside of the containment field?" Vel demanded.

Alice echoed, "Containment field?"

"Yes, containment field." Vel scowled at the liaison. "After years of trying to deal with the inhabitants of Star Cluster B, the Tri-Galactic Council decided the best way to address the problem was to create a giant containment field to keep the terror wrought by the inhabitants in one place instead of letting it spread to the rest of the galaxy and eventually the universe."

"I truly believe they are simply misunderstood," Liz Windsor persisted.

"You know," Caid said as all eyes turned toward him, "I would never speak ill of someone whose inappropriate and harmful behavior was a result of traumatic events or an emotional condition." He paused, pressed his hands together in a prayer pose, and touched his fingertips to his mouth. "But ... I would also never ask anyone to subject themselves to someone acting in a harmful or inappropriate way simply in the name of compassion or understanding."

"Meaning?" said Alice.

"Meaning, I care deeply about this crew. I worry about their—your—spiritual and emotional well-being if we deal, even in a professional sense, with an inhabitant of Star Cluster B."

Vel jabbed a thumb toward the therapist. "What more do you need to hear?"

Liz Windsor's perpetual grin was nearly extinguished. "I understand the conventional impression of Star Cluster B inhabitants is generally not favorable, but our client has already signed his contract with the Depot for this service, and he seems very sweet to me. A bit of a romantic, frankly. I do hope you'll at least reserve judgment until you meet him."

"That's all fine and good," Dan said, one eye twitching slightly, "but based on the nature of our jobs, I assume that this isn't a *single* match we're supposed to make. That's not what DeepService Team One is designed for. You might've found the only tolerable person in the entire cluster, but how do you expect us to find *any* planet willing to match and mate with a population from Cluster B?"

Liz Windsor held up her hands in a show of surrender. "It won't be easy, surely. But it's not impossible. There's a whole, big universe out there! If you want to last in this line of work, you need to believe that there exists a perfect match for every planet."

Alice had met some pretty awful people in her twenty-six years on Earth. The pastor from her hometown of Slip'n'fall, Texas, for example pulled a sneak-attack exorcism on her *twice* in her teens. One time in college, a male companion drove her to the middle of a pasture at night and left her there because she'd criticized a singer on the radio who turned out to be some guy named … Tom Yorky? She couldn't even remember. Whiny little bitch, though. Her friend and the singer.

And then there was the time in her high school chemistry class when Lindsey told everyone Alice and Matt Growski had done it at the Boyds' bonfire the weekend before. And then there was Matt Growski, who'd forced himself on her at the bonfire that one time and told her he'd kill her if she told anyone she didn't enjoy it.

Yes, she'd encountered some truly zany characters in her life, but from the way it sounded, Star Cluster B might be a touch beyond zany.

"Is there an entire planet somewhere that *deserves* to be punished?" she asked, following a winding train of thought.

Liz Windsor perked up. "Oh, I'm sure of it!" She turned to the rest of the crew. "See? Your captain has stopped saying 'can't' and has started asking 'how?' That's true leadership right there!"

Alice grinned at the others, ready to absorb praise that didn't come.

"Our client is one of the Yoken people who are the preeminent life forms on Trauna. Their planet has become inhospitable to most life, and they're running out of critical resources to sustain themselves. And, of course, their birth rate has plummeted."

"Any obvious indication of why?" Alice asked.

"I got a guess," Dan muttered darkly.

"According to the client," Liz Windsor said, ignoring him, "none is apparent. But you'll obviously want to do much more research into that." She stood. "Come. It's time you all met him for yourself. I know it will put you at ease, truly."

Vel and Caid exchanged glances—doubtful, doubtful glances—and then DeepService Team One followed Liz Windsor across the hall.

CHAPTER
THREE

"This," said Liz Windsor, holding open the meeting room door and motioning to the man sitting at the far end of the conference table, "is Aubert Orleans."

"What the …" Alice breathed, taking him in. He looked like … like a human. And what was more, he looked like a specific human: Captain America.

No, wait, she thought, *that's not the actor's real name.*

But before she could think of it, Aubert Orleans stood and shipped a charming smile her way, and any rational thinking slithered out of her ears.

Caid saw it all unfolding. It was what he'd feared. Sure, he hadn't known that the client would look so much like the captain's own species or be as symmetrical and anatomically proportionate as this one, but he'd worried that the initial charm factor of those from Star Cluster B might be a special kind of challenge for dear Alice. And now it was happening. If only he could get her into his office right that second and ask her pointed questions about her father until she saw the light!

It doesn't work that way, Caid thought. *You know it doesn't work that way. She has to come to it on her own.*

He could help lay the groundwork for a revelation, maybe poke around until something shook loose, but ultimate it was up to each person to ask the questions they need to answer for important growth. It was truly unfortunate that, in the case of Alice, the slowness of her process was incredibly likely to result in the death of everyone onboard the ship. With the exception of himself, of course. He would survive to work with another crew. Another doomed group of souls.

"You must be Captain Alice Luck." Aubert Orleans glided to the doorway where the crew had bottlenecked behind their stunned leader. He reached out, took her hand, and kissed it on the back. "It will be my honor to work with you on finding my twin flame. My people have felt incomplete for so long."

"Plesalmine," Alice dribbled.

"Why don't we all take a seat?" Liz Windsor said, grinning madly.

They did, with Alice across from Aubert, Dan and Vel on either side of her, and Caid and Liz Windsor flanking the client.

"I'm sure you're wondering about me," Aubert began, "and I don't blame you. The stories people tell about those living within my start cluster"—he exhaled in a whoosh—"I would be nervous about meeting me, too. Frankly, I'm surprised the Depot took us on as clients, considering the slander that's been spread about us throughout the universe. Awful stuff. Almost none of it true, and what little is based on fact is merely anecdotal. I hardly think it's fair to label a vast collection of planets as undesirables merely because the worst of our kind made a name for themselves, don't you?"

Alice shook her head slowly. "No, not fair at all."

"To be shut away in our galactic ghetto, ostracized, imprisoned … such unfair treatment. And for what, really?"

Vel was happy to answer the hypothetical question. "Your planet, along with fifty-eight others in Star Cluster B, participated in systematic genocide throughout the Baldonzi galaxy that resulted in six trillion deaths in four years."

Through the stark silence, Aubert narrowed his eyes. "Ah. You were a soldier, weren't you?"

Vel didn't blink. "Still am."

"I can tell. You think like one. You paint with a broad brush when you identify your enemies. Just because the worst of my planet participated in the Expansion Quest doesn't mean *I* did. And it doesn't mean the vast majority of my people did."

Liz Windsor cleared her throat. "May I remind you, Lieutenant Machiavelli, that this is our client, not a person of interest in a tribunal."

Vel didn't take her eyes off Aubert, but she said no more about the war.

"Aubert Orleans has already passed a comprehensive background check by the Depot. There were no indications in our research that he participated in the genocide that ultimately landed Star Cluster B in the containment zone. He is, however, one of the most high-ranking members of the Yoken and deserves our respect."

Aubert raised a hand. "Thank you, Miss Windsor, but I'm quite all right. This isn't the first time I've been unfairly attacked, and I'm sure it won't be the last. But I appreciate your support." He turned to Alice. "You strike me as someone who has been unjustly accused a few times. I can see the sympathy in your kind, beautiful eyes."

Alice felt herself melting under his smoldering gaze. "I—I've dealt with a sneak-attack exorcism once or twice, yes."

Aubert beamed. "You and I are going to get along just fine during this mission."

"I'm sorry," Dan said, appearing frightened as he addressed Liz Windsor. "He's not … he's not coming with us, is he?"

Liz Windsor and Aubert exchanged a conspiratorial look. "Well, yes, he is. Mr. Orleans has requested he be included in the mission."

"Um." Dan wrung his hands below the table. "Why?"

"Isn't it obvious?" Aubert said. "I mean, look at what each of you assumed about me because I'm from Start Cluster B. There's no way you could find a compatible match for someone like the people you imagine the Yoken to be. But the person I am, the way my fellow Yoken actually live their lives, that's information kept from the rest of the universe behind a wall of lies. I want you to get to know me, the real me, not the monster you believe I am."

"When you put it like that," Alice said, "it sounds like a great idea. Do we have enough room onboard *Emergence*?"

Liz Windsor's grin faltered. "Well, no. There would be plenty of room aboard *Constant*, though."

"Not happening," Alice said. "We can double up or something, but we need *Emergence*."

"Dan and I can double up," Caid offered, "seeing as how I don't take up any space. Mr. Orleans can have Dan's room. That work?"

Dan nodded quickly. "I'm thinking we'll have a lot to talk about."

Liz Windsor clapped her hands excitedly. "Oh, this is

shaping up to be quite the adventure! I'll need to move Mr. Orleans' luggage to the other ship, but that's not an issue. I'm sure you have questions for our gracious client, and his answers will allow you to determine the first destination for a possible match."

Alice took the lead. "Do you mind if I call you Aubert?"

"Not at all. Do you mind if I call you Captain?"

She giggled involuntarily. "Not at all, if that's what you prefer."

To Vel, the giggle sounded eerily like a death knell.

"Tell me about your people, Aubert. Do you have any suspicion as to what might be causing the trouble around reproduction?"

"It's not for lack of trying," he said, winking at her. "Outside of that, I can't say."

"Would you suspect it's more behavioral or genetic?"

"Neither. We're a healthy people. We engage in plenty of unprotected sex."

The Bacc'nalis had been both of those things, too, but they'd struggled nonetheless. "I'll need to learn more about the culture around sex."

"I'm happy to tell you all about it. Perhaps over a bottle of wine?"

Alice felt her cheeks heat up.

Vel apparently noticed the blush, and a sudden jab in the side of Alice's thigh pulled her back to her responsibilities.

"Usually when there's a problem," Alice said, begging her mouth not to mention livestock even a little bit in the next words she would say, "it's either behavioral or genetic. The only other option is, well, anatomical. If some event were to happen that physically disfigured a large portion of the population's genitalia, for instance."

Aubert's face darkened like a beet. "Are you implying

there's something wrong with my genitalia? How *dare* you! I ought to whip it out right here and show you how glorious it is! There's nothing wrong with me, nothing!" He smacked the table. "Don't feed me bullshit like that ever again!"

Alice blinked.

The room was silent but for the labored breathing of the client, who was on his feet, a pointed finger hardly three inches from Alice's nose.

She crossed her eyes, focusing on the digit and noting that it was trembling.

Liz Windsor was the first to speak. "Mr. Orleans, you're upset. You feel Captain Luck here has taken a cheap shot at you."

"I feel that way because she has!" But his voice was already quieter as he lowered himself back into his seat.

"I doubt that was her intent. You're going to think me a harsh, unpleasant woman, Aubert, the most insufferable *bitch* you've ever met, when you hear what I'm about to say."

His brows pinched together as he turned his attention to the liaison. "I couldn't think that about you, Liz Windsor."

"We'll see. The way you spoke to Captain Luck just now was unacceptable, and if I ever hear about you doing that again, I'll be arranging you the first transport back to Trauna, voiding our contract, and not issuing a refund."

Aubert raised his hands. "Fair enough, fair enough."

"I believe you owe Captain Luck an apology, but I'll leave that to your excellent judgment."

Aubert was slow to face Alice again, but when he did, none of the rage from a moment before could be detected anywhere in his expression. "I'm so sorry, Captain. You didn't deserve that. It would be my pleasure to make it up to you over the duration of this mission, if you'll let me. It's merely that ... Well, a man can get a bit of a persecution complex, not only being from Star Cluster B, but also being unable to do the one thing every man should be able to do: produce an heir. Sometimes the universe seems so unfair to people like me, and I get touchy. Will you forgive me?"

Everything in Alice screamed, *Run!* while at the same time, she could understand what Aubert meant. Yes, the outburst was crazytown, but he was under a lot of stress, wasn't he? Fighting his fair share of demons, as Caid might say.

She forced a smile. "Nothing to forgive."

"Excellent!" said Liz Windsor. "Then why don't we get you all settled into the ship and out of orbit? I'm sure you'll have no trouble at all scouting a good species match, and then you can head straight there."

The room got to its feet, but Alice wasn't ready to leave yet. "Hey, before we do that, any chance I could run get a slice from Franco's Pizza down the road? I'm happy to bring some back for everyone."

Liz Windsor cocked her head to the side and frowned. "Oh, I'm sorry. Franco's Pizza is closed."

"Oh, damn. What about Eastside Pizza? They never close."

"No, they're closed, too. I'm afraid all but a few restaurants in Austin are closed."

Alice blinked stupidly. "What?"

"Due to the pandemic."

"The *what*?"

"Ah yes. You were gone when all of this started. I'm afraid a sickness has swept your country. It's absolutely killing people left and right, and almost everything has shut down."

Alice, naturally quick to adapt, said, "That sucks. But we

have a spaceship. What if we pop straight over to Italy to get some—"

"No, no, no. You *definitely* don't want to go there."

Alice braced her hands on her hips. "Are you telling me there's *nowhere* I can go on this planet to get a piece of greasy pepperoni pizza right now?"

"Oh, there might be a few places open, but we can't risk your catching the virus and spreading it intergalactically."

Alice frowned. "If there's nowhere to get pizza here, then let's get the hell off this planet. Come on. I'll get Allura to cook me up something greasy. She'll love that."

CHAPTER
FOUR

"Ew," said Aubert Orleans as the next potential match appeared on the giant screen at the front of the bridge of *Emergence*. "No, she's a nasty mess. I would never mate with her."

Dan Zone was reaching the end of his rope with their new client. He extended as much generosity as he, a minister of culture, could, but his mind was involuntarily jumping frequently to his other specialty: weapons.

He glanced over at Vel, who stared unblinkingly at the screen, showing neither patience nor frustration after Aubert had nixed the ninth genetically viable match on superficial complaints alone. It wasn't like the lieutenant to tolerate this level of foolishness, though Dan had come to understand how much pride she took in being the consummate professional, just as she'd once been the consummate soldier.

And then it hit him: Vel wasn't even paying attention. In fact, she looked like she'd completely dissociated.

Lucky her.

Alice put her head in her hands. "Okay, Allura, next one."

Another female specimen appeared on the screen. Beneath her naked, rotating figure, the species stats appeared:

Location: Miragio Galaxy

Probability of genetic match: 98.7%

Average height of female: 6'4"

Average height of male: 5'3"

Sexes: 47% male, 48% female, 3% intersex, 2% herb

"How about this one?" Alice asked. "I doubt you will be able to do much with the herbs—maybe smoke them?—but your people could match with the other sexes."

Aubert rubbed his hand over his chin, squinting at the screen. Then, "Oh wait, does that say the average height of the women is six-four? Nope. Deal breaker."

"You don't want tall women?" A ball of something acidic grew in Alice's stomach.

"Not that tall. You get a woman who's that tall and she thinks she runs the place."

Alice turned on the spot. "Caid!" The therapist was lounging on the other side of the bridge, enjoying a holographic bunch of grapes. "Would you please escort Aubert into your office?"

Caid perked up, tossing the grapes, which disappeared into nothingness, and was on his feet. "He needs to talk?"

"Oh yes, I'd say he does. Maybe you can help him suss out what he's looking for in a match and then get back to us."

"Oh, absolutely." Caid ushered the client out, and Alice flopped into the captain's chair, pinching at the bridge of her nose.

Vel shook her head, blinked, looked around, then wandered over to the glass elevator. The conveyance lowered and Vel disappeared from view as Dan joined his captain in the vacant lieutenant's seat.

Alice swiveled toward him. "You understand intergalactic culture better than anyone, Dan. Tell me, if we shoved him out the door into the vacuum of space, how much trouble would we *actually* be facing?"

"Not an option. This is the first hurdle, certainly, but we'll get past it. That was smart of you to put Caid on the case of finding out more about what Aubert is into."

Alice waved that off. "Not strategic. I wanted him out. I thought I might strangle him between my thighs if I had to look at him for even a minute longer." She paused. "Everyone in Star Cluster B is like this?"

"Variations on a theme."

She scrunched her nose. "I thought he was sexy at first. Charming, too."

"If they didn't have *any* ability to pull that off, don't you think they would've been destroyed long ago?"

"I have a favor to ask of you, Dan."

He perked up. "Yes?"

"Can I leave it to you to find the right cultural match? I feel like I have my hands full worrying about finding someone *hot* enough for this asshole, let alone figuring out what's going on that's causing the infertility."

"That's why I'm here."

She leaned forward and set a hand on his knee. "Thanks, Dan. I'm glad you're on the crew."

He grinned. "How's the hangover?"

"It was on its way out after that pizza Allura made me, but now the headache's coming back on."

"Can't imagine why."

"I think I know what'll take the edge off it, though." She stood, wobbled, and braced herself on the chair. "I'm gonna shoot some guns."

The firing range was active when Alice walked into the hangar. The wall of weaponry was exposed in the holographic cave wall, and the place smelled like an automotive body shop.

Vel stood ten yards from the target portal, unloading one of the big blasters (Alice couldn't be expected to remember the names of all the various projectile weapons) into the vacuum of space.

Alice still found this setup disconcerting. The technology seemed suspect at best. Fire into God-knew-where in the universe and assume none of the blasts would hit anything that shouldn't be hit? Space was big, sure, but on her first use of the thing, an asteroid had flown past at the perfect moment to be blasted away. The odds of hitting anything were low, sure, but not zero. Never zero.

Then again, she'd done dumber and more reckless things with guns on family hunting trips and no one had died. Kenny was down a few toes, but that was hardly her fault. He should've watched where he planted hit feet while they were trying to shoot that rattler.

She grabbed a compact, short-barreled blaster from the rack and positioned herself next to Vel. "Mind if I join?"

Vel didn't pull her eyes from the target. "Nope."

Blam! Blam! Blam-blam-blam-blam!

Alice groaned as the vibrations from the kickback made her hands itch deliciously.

And now Vel was staring at her.

"What?"

"Nothing."

"Nothing?"

"Nothing, Captain."

Alice let her arm drop, aiming the blaster at the floor. Not that it would be much better to accidentally blast a hole in the floor as opposed to a wall. With regards to the vacuum of space, a big fucking hole in the ship was a big fucking hole in the ship. "Susy. Come on. I know something's been eating at you. Everyone can see it. You looked like you were having an out-of-rockin'-bod experience up there just now. What's going on? You can tell me."

For a single breath, Vel looked like she was about to spill. Then she caught herself. "It's Aubert. He's insufferable. I can't believe Liz Windsor is making us work for a Star Cluster B client."

"Okay … I feel ya on that, definitely. But you were acting up before we knew who our client was. You hardly watched the fire dancers on Jaspariampt … and they were literally fire." Alice tapped into the memory. "Wait, *were* they actually fire? Some guy with shark teeth offered me some fungus, and then things got a little wild after that. Maybe they weren't made of fire?"

"They were," Vel confirmed. "But I've seen all that before and I thought I should rest up on vacation in case our next mission wasn't as easy as the last."

"As easy? Vel." Alice leaned forward, lowering her voice. "We failed it. We failed that last one. If it hadn't been for Allura's disobedience kink that drove her to short-circuit the headquarters, we wouldn't still have this job, and we wouldn't be part of the revered DeepService Team One."

"Not One."

Alice narrowed her eyes, trying to follow along. "Right, I mean, there was a team before us that... well, *something* happened to them. Liz Windsor referenced as much. But shit happens, right?"

"And then they named us the exact same thing."

"So?"

"Almost like they're trying to pretend the past didn't happen."

Alice groaned. "If you want to be a downer about it, sure. But I think of it more like when my neighbor's German shorthair pointer got snakebit and died. She got one exactly like it, about the same age, and named it the same thing."

"You don't think that's strange behavior?"

"Now that you mention it, maybe. Is this what's got you down? The fact that we should be DeepService Team Two? I thought you *loved* being number one and hated being number two."

"It's not that. It's ... I hate Aubert."

"And like *I* said, bullshit. We *all* hate Aubert, but we're not all acting like you lately. Listen, you don't have to tell me all about it, but at least go talk to Caid. You know he gets off on all that emotional shit. If for no other reason, do it for him."

"I'll consider it. Target practice?" Vel nodded toward the portal.

"Yeah! Ooh! Do the one with the holographic ducks flying around!"

Vel reached out for the control panel and selected the setting. "They're not ducks, they're Imarnari battle drones."

"I think you're wrong about that."

"I'm not. Either way, you are good at that one."

"Psh. I'm good at all of them. I just love the noise the ducks make when you hit them. *Waaaah-booosh!* There was this guy I was hooking up with for a few weeks junior year of college who made the same noise when he ..." She noticed Vel's arched brow. "Never mind. Hit start."

CHAPTER
FIVE

Alice lay on her bed in her private cabin, browsing the files on the Yoken people. On the custom projection wall behind her, seven fire dancers gyrated and wobbled across a beach. Vel hadn't been screwing with her—it wasn't the psychedelic fungus that conjured up her belief that they were actual fire. Outer space was a wild time!

Alice swiped across the screen of her tablet, looking for more detailed schematics of the Yoken genitalia, which so far looked much like what she'd encountered in her escapades on Earth. But with the way Aubert had flipped out when she'd suggested the problem might be anatomical, she thought it warranted further looking into. After all, it was only ever the dudes with small penises who took offense to her calling them dickless.

"It's definitely small," she muttered, rotating the screen to make sure she wasn't looking at the wrong part. She'd encountered a few similarly sized parts when she went through a phase of men who watched a lot of UFC. Not unusable, but certainly nothing worth a second chance. It hadn't been the only part of those men that had made the experience less than enjoyable, though. "Allura, are the Yoken penises too small to impregnate the females?"

"No, Daddy." (Alice cringed; the pet name never sounded as fun when the topic was literal reproduction.) "The females possess short and narrow enough canals that the penis does not need to be large for the sperm to make it to the egg."

"So, what's the deal? I can't figure it out. Are the men missing swimmers?"

"I would require the live sample for that diagnosis."

"Damn. Asking Aubert for some jizz isn't my idea of a good time."

"I would hate for you to have a bad time, Daddy. Luckily, it's not necessary."

Alice perked up. "You're telling me we have a sample?"

"Yes, Daddy. Aubert Orleans provided samples immediately after he arrived at headquarters."

"Yikes. Where's HR when you need it?" She threw her legs over the side of the bed. "Has the sample been uploaded?"

"Not yet, Daddy. However, the physical samples are waiting in cold storage in your lab."

Alice tossed the tablet aside and strolled over to the other side of her chambers. Allura 4000 was a step ahead, and the wall dissolved to reveal the captain's lab on the other side.

It was only the third time she'd been inside this laboratory sober. (She might've used the available vials to pass out lemon drop shots on the way to Jaspariampt.)

Today, she would be using the equipment the way it was intended to be used: sloshing around alien cum.

She was, after all, a professional scientist.

Alice gloved up and grabbed one of the small vials of

Aubert's semen from the freezer. The cold transferred through her gloves almost immediately, and she hurried to get it over to the stand at her workstation to upload the sample to Allura. "Balls, that's *cold!*" On the last word, the bite officially hit, and reaction took over. Her pinched fingers un-pinched, and her hand took on a mind of its own, practically tossing the vial away. "Shit! Fuck!" She groped for it, trying to catch it, but she stood no chance. She winced as it clinked to the ground and rolled across the floor.

The semen sample disappeared below her stainless-steel workstation, and she paused, assessed. Could she leave it there? How long might it sit there until someone else found it and cleaned it up? "Allura, would it be a bad thing if I didn't retrieve that?"

"Yes, it will become a serious biohazard once it thaws … but you know I like being *bad*, Daddy."

Biohazard didn't sound like the right kind of bad.

Alice dropped to her knees and pressed her head to the floor to peek under the lowest shelf of the workstation. She spotted the vial all the way at the back. Angling her body toward the ceiling, she slipped her arm underneath and groped around. "Come here, you little jizz nugget …" Her tongue protruded as she strained to extend her reach a few more inches. Her fingertips found the vial, but not before her eyes landed on something written in red ink on the underside of the top shelf of the workstation. She fished out the sample, set it in a holder, then stuck her head beneath the shelf to get a better look of what was there.

The writing was in English, which she'd expected it to be, extremely Anglocentrically but not wrongly, considering the state of the universe.

She moved her lips as she read the words silently:

SC A was only the start. Do not play their game.

"South Carolina A?" she muttered. "No, that can't be it." She read it again, this time not assuming that SC meant South Carolina, because why would it? "Allura, what does this mean?"

"I'm afraid I don't know to what you are referring, Daddy. I'm just a dumb widdle baby."

"Ew. Too far. No, this writing I'm looking at. I can't make sense of it."

"I am unable to detect any writing."

"Underneath this shelf. Can you not see underneath this shelf?"

"No, Daddy. I cannot see in the traditional sense. I could run a scan of the room if you would like, but the process would irradiate all the samples, and you would be required to gain new ones from Aubert Orleans."

"Hard pass." But that got her thinking. On a ship where nothing seemed safe from the logs, she'd found somewhere that was. And someone had found it before her. But why? And what did it mean? And why was it written in red?

Or perhaps in *radical redshift.*

The permanent marker she'd selected from the job interview now lived in her bedside table. One of her few remaining possessions from Earth.

"Who used this lab equipment before me?"

"My records show that this equipment was transferred from DeepCUT *Horizon* shortly before that crew was lost."

"Lost?"

"So lost."

"Dead?"

"Fate unknown."

"Hm." Alice chewed her lip. "That was the crew before us? The real DeepService Team One?"

"No, Daddy. The equipment is from the crew that served before them."

She rolled up to sit cross-legged on the cold laboratory floor. "Wait, are we DeepService Team Three, then?"

"You are DeepService Team One."

"No, but ..." Alice lumbered to her feet, hands on her hips, gazing around at the equipment and wondering how many more messages, if any, might be found. "Never mind."

The truth was clear enough. Someone was trying to tell her something. And it probably had nothing to do with South Carolina. But after a thorough investigation, she could find no more messages written in radical redshift. There was only that one. Maybe that was all she needed.

CHAPTER
SIX

"Tell them what you told me, Aubert." Caid beamed encouragingly at the client, who seemed pleased to have all the attention centered on him once again.

The crew had gathered on the bridge after Caid announced that Aubert had experienced a few breakthroughs on what the perfect match would be for him and his people.

Alice's mind was still puzzling over the fuchsia writing she'd found in her lab, and she was only half listening as Aubert listed off the desired qualities.

That was just as well. Allura would take everything he listed, narrow the search of her database, and return possible results for Alice to review later.

Dan was paying close attention, though. He had a feeling he already knew how this would work out, and he needed to be prepared with a diplomatic suggestion when Aubert inevitably rejected everything Allura put forth. Time was ticking down on their mission, and they hadn't even left the solar system.

"Tall, but not too tall ... needs to look almost

indistinguishable from the females of my own species. She needs to be polite, but not passive, inexperienced but knows her way around the bedroom, if you get me. And she needs to want to have sex with me all of the time. She also needs to be ready to take care of things around the house, so I don't have to come back to a messy home at the end of the day. And she needs to be able to predict supernovas, obviously."

"Is that all you got, big boy?" Allura said. "Or are you gonna give me more?"

Aubert arched a brow. "If she could sound kind of like you, that would be great. I like the way you talk to me."

Vel tuned back into reality in time to catch the last half of Aubert's overly specific and literally impossible stipulations. She shot a look at her captain, hoping for a little female commiseration, but found that Alice now appeared to be taking a shift in the Land of Nowhere. The Earthling's eyes were glazed, her expression a million light years away. Huh. Being deep in thought wasn't like her.

Oh well, thought Vel before dissociating again.

"I have three matches for you within our time-space range," Allura said.

Caid gave a supportive thumbs-up to Aubert, who seemed more put out than pleased by the possibility of a match. "Fine. Let's see them."

No matter how much Dan learned about the universe, he was always pleasantly surprised when he learned more. He'd never heard of any of the three species Allura brought up, wasn't even familiar with the solar systems listed on the stat sheet that populated the right half of the screen. He knew a lot, but there was so much out there, and more every day.

"Oh, sweet void," he said when the first female specimen

appeared on screen. "Allura, there's an entire planet whose females look like *that*?" It was like seeing a goddess in the flesh. Dan made a mental note of the planet. Should he survive to retirement age, he now knew where he would look for real estate.

"Not all, Minister Zone. This is an average specimen. There is some variation."

"Naturally."

But the word had caught Aubert's attention. "Variation? Sure, *this* one isn't bad, but what if I get stuck with one on the low end? Can I see what the low end looks like?"

"I'm afraid I'm unable to pull that data for you, Mr. Orleans, as it's reliant upon subjective criteria, and I am programmed to understand that all women are equally sexy creatures whose bodies deserve to be worshipped and pleasured."

"I knew I kept you onboard for a reason," Alice said, tuning back in.

Aubert waved his hand at the screen. "Doesn't matter—she may be a five out of ten on her planet, but she's only a two on mine."

Alice jerked her head back. "You're telling me males *all over the universe* use that awful ten-point scale?"

Dan bowed his head somberly.

Aubert requested the next match, and this one, as far as Dan was concerned, was even more goddess-like than the first. The curves, the tangle of curls, the protracting claws. Hell yes!

But the client waved that one away too.

The third and final option was hardly on the screen for a second before Aubert sighed heavily and said, "I guess the DeepService Team One isn't as good as everyone says. I've seen more sexually arousing asteroids."

Alice opened her mouth, but Dan jumped in and cut her off. He'd been afraid something like this would happen, and he was starting to get a feel for Aubert Orleans. He didn't particularly like what he was feeling, but he was a quick learner when it came to speaking someone else's language. "Good work, Aubert." He clapped his hands lazily. "You've passed our test."

"I have?"

"You certainly have. Alice wasn't sure you would, but I was."

Alice scrunched up her face. "What in the flying fu—"

"The Depot has been taking on mediocre clients for years now, and the work is growing tedious. Why do you think they took on someone as interesting as you, all the way from Star Cluster B? We knew your reputation, but we didn't believe it. I, for one, assumed the rumors of Star Cluster B inhabitants arose out of jealousy rather than fact, so we devised a plan to test you and see what, precisely, the rest of the universe was so jealous of. Turns out, it's a lot, not least of which is your keen sense of taste in a mate."

Aubert's face had ballooned up with pride and superiority and looked ready to pop any second. Dan brought out the pin with his next words. "We've known all along where we'd end up. There's only one planet with enough swagger, enough clout, to please the Yoken people."

"And that is?"

"Britannica."

Pop.

Aubert gasped. "You're *kidding*. No, of course you're not. I can see it now." A sly grin spread across his face. "How long have you been searching for a match for the great ruling class of Britannica? No, don't tell me. I'm sure it's been years and years. You were waiting for someone like me to come along."

"Exactly."

Alice did her best to follow along, but Dan had lost her a while back. He was clearly pulling a fast one. She had a sixth sense for fast ones. Most of the time, she *was* a fast one. "Britannica?" she said.

Dan shot her a look that clearly said, *With all due respect, Captain, please shut your goddamn mouth on this one*, and she was happy to let that little bit of insubordination slide if it meant they could get on with this mission.

"Wow," Aubert breathed, settling into the idea of this match as easily as he would a bubbling Jacuzzi loaded up with buck-naked tens. "Can you imagine when I return to Trauna and tell them we've matched with *Britannica?*"

Dan leaned toward him. "It's going to be glorious. You'll be hailed a hero."

There were, Dan knew, a few key problems with this new plan. His gift was to spot problems coming down the wormhole, and it'd gotten him this far. It wasn't that he was able to completely stem the flow of sewage-grade fate that seemed to find him, but being covered in sewage was much better when you knew it was sewage and had been expecting the misfortune than when you didn't know what it was and hadn't seen the stank-nasty mess coming.

So, yes, this plan of his had problems. Lots of them. And while he would usually prefer to work through those problems as best he could before proceeding, he also knew when his patience was wearing dangerously thin and his cultural acumen was about to give way to his trigger fingers.

Positing Britannica was the last-ditch effort of his cultural acumen. While his captain surely wouldn't begrudge him for shooting the client if it made a big *boom* and was delivered with a fun quip or catch phrase (neither of which he had ready to go), Liz Windsor and the Depot would surely feel strongly about his rash choice.

He went the diplomatic route instead, even as he felt a tickle in both of his pointer fingers. It was unfortunate that this strategy, while certain to keep the client happy, didn't necessarily mean that the Yoken and the Britannicans would be a suitable match culturally, physically, or genetically.

But maybe …

While Aubert jabbered on in his excitement, reveling in the status he imagined for himself, Dan put his back to the others, pressed on his earpiece, and whispered, "Allura, are the Yoken and the Britannicans biologically compatible for reproduction?"

"Which Brittanican race, Minister Zone?"

He hadn't thought about that. He knew damn well who ran the place, and he'd stayed well away from them on his previous dealings with the planet. But they were the most prestigious race on Britannica now and held the most power and sway. He knew Aubert Orleans would settle for nothing less. "The splatterpoots."

Without a perceptible pause, the silky-smooth voice filled his ear. "There is a 0.00000127 percent chance of reproductive compatibility."

"Blast me to quarks," he cursed. But a single glimpse at his captain left him with a new thought, one he never would have considered prior to meeting the odds-defying woman, and one that might as easily get them killed as save them.

Ah well, maybe we'll get lucky.

CHAPTER
SEVEN

Only after Alice directed Allura to take them to Britannica via the closest space fold did Aubert finally retire to his cabin.

As soon as the client was safely out of earshot, the crew fell upon the minister of weapons and culture, demanding answers.

Vel: "What in the Shitting Seven Sisters are you thinking?"

Caid: "I would love to better understand your thoughts and feelings about this plan."

Alice: "What the hell is Britannica and why was he so excited about it?"

Perhaps because she was captain, or perhaps because hers was the most straightforward question for Dan to answer without thinking about how whopping of a mistake he might've made, he addressed it first.

"Britannica is sort of a celebrity planet."

Vel rolled her eyes so hard she had to brace herself on the back of her chair to keep from stumbling. "More like a theme park of deadly stupidity."

Alice looked back and forth between them. "I'm gonna need more information."

Dan went ahead. "It's often billed as more American than America and more British than Britain."

Alice perked up. "Oh, so I'll feel right at home there! Wait, Susy, why'd you call it a theme park of …?"

"Don't worry about it," Vel muttered darkly. "You'll feel at home, like you said."

Caid tossed a look over his shoulder to double-check that Aubert wouldn't overhear then took the extra precaution of whispering. "Dan, I'm not sure this is a good idea. Yes, it bought us some compliance from him, but when he finds out that they, like everyone else, don't want anything to do with someone from Star Cluster B … You've got to understand, he believes his emotions *are* reality. If he feels anger, there is no way to explain to him that his anger isn't one hundred percent justified and righteous to the situation, that perhaps it stems from an unfounded entitlement or a slight to his fragile ego. I don't mean to worry you, and I shouldn't even be saying this because it could be considered breaking confidentiality, but"—Caid looked around one more time—"he's *not right* in the head."

Alice reached out to pat the therapist approvingly, and her hand went straight through.

Right.

No mass, but one hell of an ass! She treated herself to a quick gander. Was it sexual harassment if no realistic threat of sexual violence was possible? She made a mental note to ponder it more fully later, but—spoiler—she never did.

"Is that an official diagnosis?" Vel asked. "'Not right in the head'?"

"Look," Alice said, tearing her eyes away from Caid's backside, "we don't *know* that this won't work out. Maybe the Britannicans will be thrilled to be matched with someone from Star Cluster B. Maybe they're, like, a perfect biological match! Allura—"

"Yes, Daddy?"

Dan's hand on her arm stopped her. "I already asked. There's a 0.00000127% chance of a match."

"See?" She grinned at the crew and felt her chest inflate with hope. "We have a chance!"

"This is a waste of time," said Vel. "A waste of time that will only end in catastrophe. We need to be looking for an actual match."

"We tried that, Susy. He shot down every one of them. At least he's excited about this. That buys us some time to figure out the next step."

"Caid's right, though," Vel persisted. "It might work for a while, but he'll be furious when he realizes that it's not a possibility, genetically speaking. Besides..." She motioned to the digital clock on the wall. Only sixty-five hours and fifty-three minutes left. "We're not exactly on vacation. We got lucky on the last mission, but we can't count on that again. We might have time for *one* planetary visit that's a bust, but we shouldn't be throwing that padding away with something we know isn't right. We'll leave no room for mistakes. And I don't know that such a thing would be strategically sound for this crew."

Alice groaned. "I need y'all to stay with me on this. You're thinking ten steps ahead, but we're not there yet. The first step is looking for some way to make Aubert happy with us, and Dan has clearly found it. Great work, Dan!" He grinned despite the growing pit of dread in his stomach. "Now we need to find another step. Then another. But *only* once we've taken the step before. Sure, we might *eventually* hit a wall, but it's only temporary. We'll find some way around. I always do. You think too far ahead, and something right in front of you smacks you upside the dome.

"Come on. We need to trust each other here." Arching a brow, she examined each of her crew members, and one by one, their expressions of trepidation gave a little.

"I'm going to let you in on a little secret about me," Alice continued. "Caid, I already know you've got a half-chub hearing me say that, but keep it in your pants. Okay, here's my secret: I do not possess the ability to think more than one, *maybe* two steps ahead. I've never played a game of chess in my life, and when people use chess metaphors like 'you're just a pawn in their scheme to get laid,' I get very confused. I admit this shortcoming has gotten me into some pickles before, but all those years of practice means I'm a pro at getting *out* of said pickles. If I wasn't, I'd have been dead long before y'all ever met me." Sensing she was losing them, she finished, "But I'm not! That's the point. I'm not dead. I'm a space captain."

"A space captain who might be dead soon," Vel muttered.

Alice didn't catch it. "Stop thinking ten steps ahead is all I'm saying. It's a pointless exercise. One step, then another, then another. That's how you walk."

"It's also how you run screaming from a Vervi Girthworm whose nest you've stumbled into," Vel added, and this time Alice did catch it.

Alice put her fists on her hips defiantly. "You know what, Susy? I haven't a goddamn clue that a Pervy Girthworm is, but it sounds like an adventure. It's all about how you frame it, right, Caid?"

Caid's mouth hung open as he shook his head slightly. "Um, yeah, I guess."

She jabbed a finger at the therapist. "See? Caid agrees. What do y'all say? Do you trust me to lead us one step at a time?" She flopped her palm into the middle of the unwitting huddle.

Dan was the first to speak. "Yes, Captain. I trust you."

"Great." She nodded toward her outstretched hand. "You put yours on top."

"Why?"

"I'm teaching you American culture, Dan, and you ask *why*?"

He quickly put his hand on top of hers.

"That was a fascinating moment of self-reflection, Alice, along with an admirable demonstration of appreciation for the skills you possess." Caid put his useless holographic hand on top of Dan's.

Alice turned to Vel. "What do you say, Susy?"

"This is stupid and likely to get us killed if we don't accidentally start an intergalactic war."

"Come on." Alice nodded again toward the middle. "Hand in. I'll buy you some Dippin' Dots when we land."

"Dippin' Dots?"

"If this Britannica place really is anything like America, they have 'em. Hand in, please."

And Vel, hoping that Dippin' Dots was something worth dying for, begrudgingly put her hand in.

Alice launched the pile of hands into the air. "Hell yeah! Here we come, Britannica!"

CHAPTER
EIGHT

Our universe is by nature a violent place. The composition shakes out to fifty percent violence and fifty percent *Oops! Things-got-a-little-out-of-hand-so-let-me-make-it-better-through-gravity-and-distance-and-such*. The "me" in that is, of course, the same "me" as the reason your wife left you.

It's a place of explosions, our universal bubble. A furnace and then—oopsies!—a freezer to make up for it.

Fifty percent of it is complete accident, and the other fifty percent is intentional, but no one knows which part is which, so it all amounts to the same thing: you are very lucky to be alive at any given moment.

The equal odds of violence and nonviolence aren't spread evenly through space-time. There are pockets of ultra-violence and pockets of boring nonviolence. It may not surprise you to learn that within those pockets of nonviolence are the best places for life to spring up.

However, *too much* life and violence tends to arise. Life always finds a way.

It was in one of these pockets of temporary nonviolence that Blerg VFP69 existed and began generating violence.

Shortly after, relatively speaking, these little Homo sapiens dickheads began launching themselves off the planet. That was the opposite of a chill vibe, especially once some of them never returned to Blerg VFP69.

One such dickhead was named Charles Milton Strumpkins, because of course he was. Strumpkins was born in Atlantic City, New Jersey, United States, and then moved to a place called Lubbock, Texas, United States, where he studied aerospace engineering, but not well. During his studies, he spent a semester in Oxford, England, United Kingdom. Strumpkins returned from that time feeling rather worldly and superior, and no one in Lubbock ever stopped hearing about it.

Until, that is, Strumpkins finally launched himself off the planet, which brought much joy to those still on it.

Very few people ever knew that he'd launched himself off the planet. Most people who noticed his absence said things like "Mouth finally wrote a check his ass couldn't cash," or "Who gives a flying fuck where that pompous bullshitter is? He ain't here, and that's all that matters."

But Charles Milton Strumpkins was simply hurtling through the vacuum of space in a vessel he had very little control over, jumping space folds like it was Double Dutch. He was Jersey, he was Texas, he was England, he was Blerg VFP69, and he was traveling faster than light!

When he finally landed on a planet, received approval from his low-tech instruments that the atmosphere wouldn't immediately kill him, then set foot on the strange new world, his first thought was *I'm gonna make this place my bitch.*

From a *somewhat* violent planet to a *mostly* nonviolent one had traveled a (relatively) tiny bomb of *absolute* violence. He killed the first three beings he encountered when they looked at him like he was stupid rather than Oxford educated for a semester. He fucked the next being because it was giving him bedroom eyes (its eyes always looked like that, and bedrooms didn't exist on the planet yet). He shouldn't have done it, not only for obvious moral reasons, but because the thing was incredibly toxic and, unbeknownst to him, had left behind millions of microscopic needles in his offending genitals. But those wouldn't manage to kill him for a few agonizing months. In the meantime, he sent a message to Blerg VFP69 that doomed what would later be named Strumpkins BAP1.

The message said, "This place rocks. Send *way* more people."

Time is a complicated thing, even before space folds get involved, and by the time the next crew arrived, Strumpkins was hardly more than bones. No one from the Depot had explained to him how time worked. It was their policy not to.

In the months that Strumpkins was still alive, while his penis was being dissolved from the inside out by the tiny toxic needles, though he'd by no means managed to make the place "his bitch," he had managed to leave his unfortunate cultural mark on it. When the full Depot crew arrived, they were greeted by incredibly peaceful (though understandably wary after that one dickhead) beings that grinned, waved, and said, "Howdy, gov'nah."

Alice went with a bright red jumpsuit to match her Texas flag boots. She hadn't realized how much she'd missed the familiarity of her home planet until the thought of arriving on a similar one seeped into her mind's eye.

Would all the things she loved most be there? Would they have football and barbecue? Could Dairy Queen and ZeigenBock have made it this far from Earth? It seemed unlikely, sure, but *she'd* made it this far, so nothing was impossible.

The list of things she missed kept growing longer in her mind as she met the others in the hangar of the ship. Once this mission was complete, hopefully that virus thing Liz Windsor said was going around Earth would've passed, and Alice could enjoy some of her homeland's delights once again. Pizza, sure, but also bonfires, bluebonnets, and maybe some hog wrestling.

Emergence touched down at the planet's main port of entry as Alice took a quick vibe check of her crew. Dan, dressed in a white crew shirt and navy-blue slacks, bounced anxiously on his heels, which she noticed had a pair of red Jordans on them. At least he took his job seriously.

Vel stared at the hangar port with laser eyes but an otherwise expressionless face. It was a look that reminded Alice of the jungle camouflage she'd seen on soldiers in Vietnam movies; no visible threat, but something deadly waited beneath.

Caid had his eyes closed, his palms pressed together at what Alice had learned against her will during their vacation was his heart chakra. (He'd never trick her into a sunrise meditation session again.)

Aubert's spine could not have been straighter. He'd rolled his shoulders so far back, chest puffed, that she thought the tips of his shoulder blades must be touching.

Oh boy. Maybe this *was* a bad idea. The man had ballooned up in every possible way—physically, emotionally, egotistically—and that meant a single, gentle pinprick might be enough for him to pop.

Let's hope this works.

The doors opened, and a greeting committee of strange-looking but friendly bipedal creatures was already waiting.

"Welcome to Britannica!" said one resembling a kangaroo. It hopped toward Alice, holding out a string of multicolored beads, and the captain bowed her head to let it slip them on her. She thanked the greeter and looked down at the string across her chest. She'd earned similar ones at Mardi Gras, but these were substantially duller in color and had required less public exposure. And then a long-ago memory surfaced, and she gasped. "Are these *edible?*"

The kangaroo thing nodded enthusiastically. "Most definitely. Enjoy your stay on Britannica."

"Oh, I have a feeling I will." She placed a bead between her molars and chomped. Hints of strawberry and chalk. Phenomenal.

From beside her, Vel, who accepted her beads out of courtesy, tucked them into one of her navy-blue jumpsuit's pockets and sniffed the air. "I can smell the adrenaline of this place."

Alice sucked hard on the candy pieces as they dissolved on her tongue. "Isn't it great?" The rest of the capital city was visible up ahead, and she was eager to explore. It was unfortunate that they had an appointment with the president in just over an hour, because she'd had Allura list some of the main attractions of this place, and it seemed like somewhere she'd happily drop money on, somewhere that offered an "all-inclusive" option at a reasonable price.

"Follow me, Aubert," she said to the grinning client, and then the crew, plus one, set out down the walkway toward the bright and busy city of Washington, U.K.

Vel knew a dangerous environment when she saw one. The sticking point for most people—not her, though—was that the deadliest places tended to look quite inviting. If the place was known to harbor murderous beasts or, void eat them all, saber-toothed fungi, then a person *knew* to keep their eyes open and legs ready to run.

It was the places that tried the hardest to seem friendly that were almost always the most inhospitable to a long and happy life, and Britannica, which she knew by reputation, was such a place if she'd ever set foot on one.

Alice, obviously, was enamored. Her mouth hung open as they entered the city and took in the full glamor of the place.

No, the captain couldn't be relied upon here. Vel would have to be the eyes and ears.

"Susy! They have fast food, Susy! Dan! Can you believe? This place is so goddamn *cultural!*" Alice weaved back and forth down the sidewalk of the busy avenue while Vel prepared to grab her if she darted in front of one of the personal transports zipping by, which seemed likely.

A leash. A leash would be useful.

Alice's brain struggled to process all the familiar yet novel input. It was like being at home but without all the crappy parts like student loan payments, humane society commercials, and possibly running into an ex.

The city was a swirl of bright colors splashed across rotating restaurant signs, retail stores, and laser tag at every block. None of the franchises were familiar, but each was a close estimation of something that Alice *had* seen before.

Wedged between a MacBeth's Donuts and a Mach-1 Drive-in Burgers, a neon-orange water slide spat one small being after another into a shallow pool. And beyond that, a spiny creature slithered out of a Pizza Hovel with a large, squirming sack slung over one shoulder and a stack of no fewer than fifteen cardboard boxes balanced on the tiny suckers of a tentacle tip. When the smell from those boxes met Alice's nostrils, her arms temporarily turned to jelly. "Peeeeeezzaaaa," she moaned.

While the knockoffs were plentiful and a suitable stopgap, there was one brand that *had* made it all the way out to Britannica, and spotting it restored the use of her limbs. "Vel! Can you believe it, Vel? It's Dippin' Dots! I knew they'd be here! I told you! Oh, Aubert, you have to try them!"

The client from Star Cluster B was similarly stumbling, though not stunned so much by the feeling of home and the visual stimulation as he was enjoying an overwhelming rush of self-importance. He orgasmically imagined how much praise he would receive when he returned to Trauna to report that he *and he alone* had managed to get his people matched with those of Britannica. His name would live forever!

"It's incredible," Aubert replied, his chin high, brain light. Yes, the people of Britannica would all learn to love him, no doubt. They would probably erect a statue of him in their square, wedged between a novelty sundae shop and a go-cart track. *"Who's that, Mommy?"* a small boy would ask, stumbling from a go-cart and pointing to the glorious statue. *"That's the savior of our people, stupid little boy. How dare you not know who that is. I didn't raise you to be this ignorant. This must be your father's doing. Your ignorance is why I took up with that beautiful Trauna man. In a lot of ways, your ignorance was why your worthless father and I got a divorce. That's Aubert Orleans, and don't you forget it or I'll kill you in your sleep!"*

Caid, meanwhile, took in the overstimulating surroundings with a sense of detached concern. He'd explored plenty of psyches that much resembled the city of Washington, U.K. This place was the physical manifestation of a life unexamined, of unhealthy cycles that, while fun, led to nowhere and only compounded, shrinking the world, narrowing the range of possibilities. This was a city spiraling the drain, a civilization of sound and fury and dopamine hits. There would be a lot to unpack with his crewmates after this visit. And he was sure they had yet to see the full spectrum of horror, too.

Vel, at least, didn't appear to be buying into it, and Dan, while an interested student of the culture, also appeared to be approaching the allure with a healthy level of skepticism, despite an obvious desire to let go and indulge.

If only Caid could say the same for the captain and the client.

While Alice had demonstrated annoyance at Aubert on *Emergence*, those natural protective instincts seemed to have thinned to nothing in this new environment. The two were now arm in arm, skipping down the sidewalk.

"Do you even know where we're going?" Vel asked, hurrying to keep up.

"I know where *I'm* going," Alice said. "There's one of those zero-gravity rides over there! It spins you and you get pressed to the wall and you can lift up your feet and—"

Vel had spotted the thing already, but had noted it as a potential threat, not a way to kill time. "The Spaghettificator?" she said incredulously.

"Yeah!"

"If I'd known you were into that, I would've told Allura to steer *Emergence* straight into the nearest black hole. Would save us a lot of trouble with the Depot. We're here for a reason, remember, Captain?"

Alice detached herself from Aubert, who didn't seem to

notice, and threw her free arm around the lieutenant. "Susy. Vely. Baby. I'm trying to show our client a good time."

Caid injected himself. "You may believe that's what you're doing, but you're merely inflating his ego instead."

"And?" Alice said. "He enjoys that. It seems to be his only passion."

"But it never ends well," Caid replied. "Ego inflation isn't the answer to anything."

"I'll be honest, bub, I don't truly have a handle on what the word 'ego' means, but you usually have sound arguments." Alice sighed. "Fine, where do we need to go?"

"Our meeting is in Little Texas," Vel explained, despite the fact that Alice should've already known that after their team brief. "We're scheduled to meet with the president and queen to discuss the possible match."

Alice's pupils dilated. "Little Texas? Why didn't you tell me? Will they have Dippin' Dots, too? What am I saying? Of course they will! Okay, I'll wrangle Aubert."

She was plenty happy to follow Vel's lead, via Allura's instructions, to their destination. It freed her up to take in more of this wonderful place. Every sight triggered an association, a memory from a land far, far away. The real Texas.

The real home.

The experience took on a bittersweet taste before she knew it, and she absent-mindedly nibbled on another candy bead to sweeten things up again. It didn't work.

With every fresh drop of recognition, her unexpected longing for home intensified. Despite how little she had liked things prior to hopping aboard Liz Windsor's transit from that rooftop to escape an engagement that would've been survivable *at best*, there was still something crucial to the familiar. Hoping it would be an antidote, she assured herself that the truly familiar still existed and she could pay it a visit later on, after this mission and another vacation, even though it was torture to stay at home for long.

Alice had never been to Times Square, but she'd watched a few Spider-Man movies in that phase during her junior year of college when she'd decided nerds were sexy. The deeper she got into Washington, U.K., the more it reminded her of the Spider-Man movies. Tall signs reaching high, flashing, imploring you to consume; entire buildings whose sides were screens where strange-looking species brawled and shouted at each other or were handed awards or critiqued by a panel of other strange species.

God, she missed reality TV. There had never been enough of it on those nights when her friends were busy studying and she'd been left with nothing but her useless thoughts.

Here on Britannica, though, she might finally get her fill of it. Nonstop reality TV beat nonstop reality any day of the week.

They turned onto a street called Audition Boulevard, and she saw right away how it'd earned its name. Every building was set back significantly from the street to allow for the long, winding lines leading up to large casting-call signs. But casting for what?

Who cares? she thought. *I could be famous! Then I'd never have to work a job again!*

But wait, didn't she already have enough money to never work a job again? And here she was. Why? With the musky promise of fame so thick in the air, she struggled to remember.

It wasn't easy to navigate the crowded sidewalks, and she lost track of Vel twice, only to have the woman's hand appear between crowded bodies to grab her by the jumpsuit collar and tug her forward.

By the time the crew of DeepService Team One made it off Audition Avenue, Alice was relieved to escape the bustle that she had initially found exhilarating.

A man who resembled something she'd seen swimming in the deep sea on a nature documentary while she was high approached her, wearing a headdress. "You're a very pretty woman. Very pretty. You deserve one of these." From his arms dangled a heap of colorful, feathered head dresses, which he shook at her. "Pretty lady deserves a pretty headdress."

Alice cringed. "Yikes, even *I* know that's racist. No thanks."

The vendor appeared genuinely stunned. "No offense. I mean no offense. Your head is naked, and I thought to cover it."

"Yeah, but those are, like, cere … monial?" She deferred to Dan, who nodded.

"Yes, yes," the vendor insisted. "The great ceremony. I have most respect. You know of the pilgrimage, then."

"Eh, I don't think 'pilgrim' is the word you wanna use here."

Dan intervened. "Hold on. What pilgrimage?"

"To the holy site," said the vendor. "On America, each youth on the precipice of independence selects a headdress to show who they will become. Then they begin yearly pilgrimage to the sacred gathering of Coachella."

"Oh boy," said Alice. "Okay. That's"—she whistled low—"that's not good." She grabbed Dan's arm and quickly led him away. "What a fucking bummer *that* is. The guy's got it all wrong." She paused. "Wait. Is that cultural appropriation? Is he culturally appropriating … Who the hell is he culturally appropriating there? I'm ..." She blinked, trying to grasp it, then shook her head. "Why am I upset that Britannica has culturally appropriated our cultural appropriation?"

"Almost there," Allura announced breathily in everyone's ear. "So close, just a little more ..."

They passed a restaurant called Flip the Table that announced on a large sign that it was "The #1 place in Washington, U.K. to host your epic public meltdown! Film crew included when you buy 3 large pizzas!"

Vel shot it a look of disdain. "How this planet hasn't been brutally conquered yet ..."

But Alice made a note of the location. She'd always wanted to flip a table in public.

CHAPTER
NINE

It was glaringly obvious where the boundary of Little Texas began.

Vel, leading the group, was the first to spot it and said, "What."

Grabbing Aubert by the shoulders and shaking him, Alice declared, "We're here! We've made it to Texas!"

"Didn't you spend your whole life in Texas?" Vel asked. "Liz Windsor said you hopped on the ship to skip town as soon as she offered you the job. Doesn't sound like someone who wants to stay in Texas."

Alice blew a raspberry. "That situation is much more nuanced than you're making it out to be. But this ... it's like being at the state fair."

There was, in fact, no more accurate way to describe it. The perimeter of Little Texas was marked by old wooden stakes strung with barbed wire. (Though it didn't look it, the barbed wire was incredibly electrified.) This was presumably to keep alien versions of cattle within the boundaries, but also to make sure those who entered were forced to proceed through the two giant cowboy sentries standing watch on either side of the entrance.

Unlike the famed Big Tex statue that Alice had tipped her hat to at the state fair many times, these fifty-foot-tall beings weren't statues. Though whether they were organic beings or organic holograms, she wasn't sure. Maybe she could give one a poke to find out.

Before she could act upon that impulse, however, a small being with two useful legs and six fragile, bug-like legs, said, "Look, Mama!" then did the poking on Alice's behalf. Without otherwise acknowledging the child, the giant cowboy's leg kicked out and send the curious child flying through the air, above the crowd. She didn't see where the being landed.

"Geesh." She cringed up at the cowboy, who spun a lasso lazily above his heads and said things to those passing by like, "Howdy, yeehaw partner," "What in the Sam Hill of beans?" and "Them there, y'all!"

Alice leaned toward Dan as they approached the gates. "For the record, those aren't things we say. They don't even make sense. Oh, also, don't poke them."

"Noted. But I'm not surprised the sayings are wonky. You do, of course, realize that we're over four hundred light-years away from the real Texas, don't you?"

"No, I wasn't aware of the distance, and I'm still struggling with what a light-year is exactly."

"It's the distance light travels—"

Alice held up a hand. "Don't bother."

"My point is that we're far from *your* Texas, so I suspect most of what we're about to see and hear will not be true to the original culture. Distance is the enemy of communication."

Alice frowned, already feeling disappointment seeping in. "Will they at least have tacos?"

"Oh yes, I suspect they'll have plenty of tacos. Most places do, if you can figure out the local word for it. Tacos have pretty much made their way through the entire universe. There's a great taco truck on Lavost, actually. I'll have to take you there sometime if we get another vacation. Homemade spleen tortillas."

She stuck out her tongue. "You weren't kidding about the lost-in-translation thing."

Dan stuck his nose into the air. "It's called Colonial fusion, Captain."

Alice ignored the condescension as they reached the back of the line to get into Little Texas. On the horizon she saw a Ferris wheel, and her mind traveled back to seventh grade, when Tucker King had kissed her right on the mouth while they dangled forty feet in the air in their rickety bucket made for two. His lips had been tinted blue from the cotton candy they'd shared, and tasted of it, too. The sweetest kiss in all meanings of the word.

Tucker King. Wow, she hadn't thought about him in years, and suddenly a part of her ached. But why the ache? What did it mean?

"Howdy, y'all horny toads!"

The deep bass of the sentry's greeting rattled her bones when she was this close to it. She flinched at the words for a handful of reasons.

But then they were inside. They'd crossed the border into Little Texas.

"Here you go, ma'am," said a possum-like being inside the gate. Alice turned, and the creature pressed a blaster into her hands, no questions asked.

"I already have one, thanks," Alice replied.

"Then take another!"

"No, I have another. I'm pretty well armed. Is that a problem?"

"In Little Texas, the only problem is if you're *unarmed!*" The possum grinned eerily, its eyes glassy, pupils dilated. "Or if you're trying to cross the border ... illegally."

"Um." Alice cringed but accepted the blaster so she could stop talking to the mangy maniac.

"We're not going to make it out of here alive, are we?" Vel said, her eyes darting from person to person in the crowd.

Alice inspected the weapon in her hand. "They're not real blasters, right? They can't be." It looked like a six-shooter, but the possum has said "blaster," and blasters didn't use bullets, so maybe it was a toy.

"No, they're real," Vel assured her.

"How can you tell?"

The lieutenant raised hers into the air and pulled the trigger. A burst of blue light shot from the barrel and kept going, into the wide-open sky.

"Yeeehaaaw"s rose up from the crowd, and without a moment's pause, dozens of blasters aimed toward the sky and fired. More yeehaws followed. More blasts followed that.

"Vel," Alice said, as an uncharacteristic crease of concern appeared between her brows. "You see that creature over there? The small, hairy one with the antennae next to the two bigger ones. Is that a *child?* And it's got its own *blaster?*"

Dan poked his head into the conversation. "That's an adult dwarf Glauster'ral. But that"—he pointed to a walking stick of a being—"is a young Traffft. Developmentally equivalent to, say, a three-year-old child."

"And they gave it a blaster upon entry?" Alice asked.

"Hmm," said Dan. "Either that or it brought its own."

Alice looked around, finding herself in the novel position of feeling uncomfortable around guns. "That's very young to be giving someone a weapon. I didn't get mine until I was seven, and even then, it was just a .22. Hardly a gun at all. Someone's going to *die* from this."

"Most assuredly," Dan replied. "The death rate in Little Texas is quite extraordinary. That's why they keep a daily tally. But when you chat with the locals, which I have, you'll find that the practice of young blaster ownership comes from deeply held values of individual freedom and personal responsibility."

"You gotta respect that," said Aubert Orleans, inserting himself into the conversation.

"No, we don't," snapped Vel. "It's sociopathic."

Aubert harrumphed. "Maybe that kind of attitude is why *your* people aren't a perfect match for those of Britannica."

"Yeah," she said. "That's probably why."

Alice nervously nibbled on her necklace before letting it fall back to her chest. "I'm with Vel here. I love me some individual freedom, like, I *love* it, but I don't see how that amounts to babies with six-shooters."

As pleased as Vel was that her captain was finally showing some sense, she knew better than to sit and bask in it. Not with this many armed toddlers bunching up at the entrance. Best to get a little space between the crew and everyone else.

She placed a hand on Alice's back. "We'd better get going, Captain. Don't want to be late to meet the president."

CHAPTER
TEN

By the time they reached the capitol, Aubert had managed to get a hold of five more blasters and a shoulder holster that could hold up to twenty blasters of various sizes; Caid had talked Dan through three small fits of the quantum jitters after rogue blasts had only missed him due to a well-timed stumble, a sneeze, and a dirty joke about sheep from his captain that had caused him to stop in his tracks to figure out if he'd heard her right; and Vel was wondering what her life would've been like if she'd been booted to literally any other parallel universe but this one.

"You think they'll have snacks for us?" Alice asked as they scaled the capitol steps. "I just passed up more fried food than I thought possible. Deep-fried beef and macaroni pizza? Come on! Truly a heroic culinary act."

"I'm sure they'll have food, Captain," Dan assured her. "For what it's worth, I'm hungry, too."

"Guess the jitters take it out of you, huh? But, hey, at least you're in a reality where you live to eat another meal!"

"Don't speak too soon," Vel muttered. "Still a chance we

could be killed by a stray blast or a rowdy game of Stand Your Ground."

"I get that you don't love it here, Susy, but Stand Your Ground looks pretty fun." The game had reminded Alice a little of one she used to play, King of the Hill, which was essentially an all-out slugfest to be the one standing at the top of a pile of hay bales. And once you were up there, your only job was to fight off the others. The game ended when the first person cried *and* had an injury to show for it. Skinned knees and broken bones that failed to poke through skin didn't count.

Stand Your Ground, the name of which was displayed on the ticket booth outside the small, fenced-in area, was similar to her childhood pastime in that it involved balance and dodging attacks. But instead of fighting hand to hand, each participant stood on a bale of hay and chucked beanbags from a bucket at the others, hoping for a head shot that knocked them off. It was, by far, the safest activity Alice had seen since entering Little Texas.

Or it would've been, were it not for the barbed wire covering the ground around each bale.

Two bipedal beings who were head to toe in black and shamelessly wearing Zorro masks stepped forward when DeepService Team One reached the doors to the capitol.

"Greetings, fine Little Texans!" Alice said, hesitating after remembering that she'd only casually scanned the cultural brief Dan had provided her about Little Texans and Britannicans at large. Damn. Crossing her fingers that there weren't any sounds she wasn't allowed to use, she forged ahead with confidence. "My name is Captain Alice Luck, and we're DeepService Team One. We're here on invitation of the president and queen."

"*Sí*, Capitan Luck. *Bienvenido al capitolio.*" Bowing, they pulled open the doors.

"The hell he say?" asked Aubert, glaring at the one who'd spoken as he passed.

"It's Spanish," Alice said. "It's a language commonly spoken in Texas. Be cool. They welcomed us."

Thank you, Spanish electives.

It took a moment for Alice's eyes to adjust to the dimmer light, and she blinked away the darkness until she was able to behold the grandeur ahead. "It's the rotunda!" She grabbed whoever was closest to her, which happened to be Dan after her hand swiped straight through Caid and dragged him forward through the empty and cavernous space of the capitol building.

"Look up," she said, and he did.

Above them was a beautifully painted ceiling of a dome, the letters T-E-X-A-S in a tight circle at the center. Alice spun him along with her. "It's not a visit to the capitol if you don't spin in the middle." She stumbled out of her spin and waved for the others to join.

Vel's hand inched toward her hip holster. "No thanks."

Before Alice could press the issue, two servants in woven ponchos and sombreros appeared from a hallway, carrying two steaming platters.

"El Presidente wishes for us to bring you this meal prior to the meeting."

Narrowing her eyes at it through her self-imposed dizziness, Alice gasped and cupped her hands to her mouth. She stumbled a step to her left.

"What?" Dan said, beginning to panic and wishing to the universe she hadn't made him dizzy prior to facing some sort of adversary. "What is it?"

"Are those... tacos?" Alice asked.

"*Sí*, Capitan. Double-decker."

Taking a taco in each hand seemed like the appropriate thing to do, so that was what she did, encouraging the others to grab theirs from the platters as well. Aubert was more than happy to help himself, but the others, sans Caid, who obviously couldn't indulge, showed more hesitancy. Some might've even called it discretion, or perhaps wisdom.

Alice gave them the stink-eye until they gave in.

Vel made sure to carry it away from her body to avoid the grease drips, and in her nondominant hand.

"This way," said one of the servants. "El Presidente *y* Her Majesty are ready to speak with you. *Vamos*."

"They keep using these words I don't know," Aubert whined around a mouthful of taco meat. "I don't like it. Don't these workers know Universal English? They should have to learn it."

While Dan didn't fully agree with this take, he, too, was finding himself lost on the new language. "You said it's Spanish?" he asked as the poncho-ed men led them toward a door at the edge of the rotunda.

"*Sí*," Alice replied, sending a chunk of ground beef—or whatever the hell this meat was (she didn't care)—shooting from her mouth and landing on the marble floor a few feet ahead of them. She crushed it under her boot a second later. "That means yes in Spanish."

"You know Spanish?" Dan asked.

"*Un poco*," she said. "That means a little. Took two years of it in high school and two more in college. Never thought I'd use it, let alone in a situation like this." She gestured with her taco at the getup of those leading them down the hall. "That's racist, by the way. I mean, yeah, Mexicans used to wear that, but not all of them. And they don't anymore except in, like, resort towns, but I think they're forced to wear it. Or maybe it earns them better tips. Either way, I knew plenty of Mexicans in College Station, and when my buddy Justin dressed like that for Halloween, they let him know it was racist by getting him kicked out of student government. The next year David—he was a Mexican—David dressed as a Justin. Dickies and a polo shirt, went around hitting on girls who were clearly not interested, and called everyone 'brah' and 'homie.' Very white." She glanced at Dan. Was he impressed? She may not have pored over the Britannica brief, but she didn't need one to know about Mexicans and white guys. Finally, she had the cultural upper hand. "Hey, how come you didn't know about Spanish? Haven't you been to Britannica before?"

"Oh yes. How do you think they got their hands on so many blasters?"

Alice narrowed her eyes. "I assumed they made them somewhere. Maybe a Little Tennessee?"

Dan laughed. "Does this seem like a planet with skilled armorers? No. Like most people in the universe, they bought their stock from the Ministry of Weapons and Culture."

She wiped the grease from her hand onto her jumpsuit. "You're an arms dealer?"

"Sometimes, yes."

"Remind me who you work for?"

"The Ministry of Weapons and Culture."

"No, no. I get that. But *who* runs that?"

"Oh." Dan chuckled. "An intergalactic coalition."

"Coalition of what?"

"Corporations."

"What kind of corporations?"

"Subsidiaries of the Depot, mostly."

Alice crinkled her nose. "And this is the first time you've encountered Spanish?"

"Yes, the Mexican culture was missing last time I visited. The guards wore chaps and cowboy hats."

"And how were the tacos last time?"

He shrugged. "Not as good."

"That's how it goes. We tried to take Mexico out of the tacos back in Texas, too. Doesn't work. I don't know why, but it's impossible. You end up with carrots and kale and shit in them. It just appears. You want good tacos? You need people speaking Spanish. Guess El Presidente figured that out."

"That's why you think they're speaking Spanish? For the tacos?" He chomped another bite of his.

"Probably not."

"Then why?"

"Texas was Mexico before it was the United States. You take the Mexico out of it, and all you're left with is … well, I don't know. Football? Dallas affluenza?"

Dan nudged her playfully, absolutely high as a kite on grease. "I'm learning so much from you, Captain."

"Plenty more genius insight where that came from." She winked.

From up ahead: "Almost there, *señores y señoritas.*"

Alice licked the grease from her fingers and rolled her shoulders back. Game time.

At the end of the long hallway, the men in ponchos announced the arrival of DeepService Team One as they opened the doors and motioned for the crew to step inside.

The cavernous room was bipolar. The décor reminded

Alice of when her brothers Buck and Charlie taped a line straight down the center of their shared bedroom—the electrician's tape traveling up onto the walls and ceilings, even, so there was no ambiguity about whose side was whose. They even split the doorway in half, so they could come and go without stepping a toe over the line.

Half of this space reminded Alice of an ornate tearoom or a set stolen from *Masterpiece Theater*, which her film-buff hookup liked to talk all the way through. Large-patterned wallpaper covered that hemisphere of the room, and a series of expensive and no-doubt uncomfortable wing-backed chairs and love seats established a handful of sitting areas with delicately carved side tables completing the look. She could practically see Winston Churchill sitting on one of those benches, smoking a cigar and regaling a small audience with his best tales.

Unbeknownst to anyone, least of all Alice, when she conjured up Winston Churchill in her mind, who she was actually imagining was Wilford Brimley. And he would've seemed more at home on the *other* half of the bipolar room.

Because the other half was quite the one-eighty, but she found it a much more familiar aesthetic on the whole. Along the wood-grained walls, dozens of glassy-eyed faces stared at her, each mounted one right after the other. Not deer or bears or coyotes or bobcats, but strange alien beasts with too many eyes and head shapes so strange they could've been the backsides and Alice wouldn't have known the difference.

Beneath the zombie audience were small sitting spaces comprised of overstuffed tanned leather couches with decanted amber liquid and crystal glasses on each of the sturdy side tables. Blaster racks stood in rows along the walls, wherever the mounted heads allowed the space, and dried hides with baffling fur patterns lay like the elegant roadkill they were across the hardwood floor. She thought Wilford Brimley would look at home in a setting like that, swirling the liquid in his glass, telling a hunting-weary group about the time he faced off with a lion. Of course, the face she conjured when imagining Wilford Brimley was, strangely enough, Karl Marx.

And on the far side of the room, not to be overlooked, were two large thrones, one built like a shoe-shining station, the other much more like what Alice imagined a throne *should* look like, with ornate metal patterns and a large red cushion. And atop each of these thrones sat, respectively, El Presidente and Her Majesty the Queen. Neither was particularly humanoid.

The president rose from his chair, as if DeepService Team One had simply caught him in a candid moment of sitting on a throne and doing nothing at all, and descended the small set of steps, his tentacles massaging their way along, the spurs on the tip of each jangling with every invertebrate quiver.

Alice looked to Dan for a sign of what to do. She knew enough about octopuses to know you didn't fuck with them, but the president wasn't *exactly* an octopus—for example, he had about fifteen legs, and she didn't know the Greek or Roman root for fifteen—so it was unclear to her what their threat level truly was.

Dan was her best gauge of that, and since he didn't look too disturbed by the form of the president, Alice relaxed and decided to roll with the whole jelly-man thing.

But here's the problem: Dan wasn't *all* fight or flight. Sometimes, when the threat was especially high, he was freeze, and unbeknownst to Alice, this was one of those times.

Dan was, in fact, screaming on the inside. Knowing ahead of time that the planet was governed by splatterpoots and finding himself face to face with them were two separate things. He'd successfully managed to avoid their kind on previous visits and had been quite thrilled with that. But no longer.

Stay cool, Dan. This was your idea, and the last thing you need is for the rest of the crew to show fear. Splatterpoots squirt themselves over that.

He forced a placid expression and hoped no one else on the crew had any idea what they were up against.

The queen wasn't much more comforting of a sight, but we'll get to that in a second.

"Welcome! I hear we have a gen-u-ine Texan in our midst!" El Presidente held out a few tentacles to the group as he undulated his way over.

Alice was not especially well versed in American history, but she was pretty sure the president's ensemble was closer to a mood board than an outfit. He appeared to have a few tentacles dedicated as legs—on those he wore the spurs—and others dedicated to being arms—at the tips of those, he'd slipped on stiff, leather-like gloves with the fingers, all six of them, clearly stuffed and inoperative. Like a puppet's hands. She counted seven hands and five legs, but the legs were extremely hard to keep track of as they wobbled around, and she wouldn't have been surprised to learn she'd missed some and double-counted others.

He wasn't *all* tentacles, which was a thought Alice never realized could bring such relief. Much like the octopuses she feared back on Blerg VFP69, the president had a knobby thing sticking up from the center of the nightmare nest of limbs, and while it flopped around ever so slightly, the top of it was clearly where the talking came from. Above his

Confederate jacket, a red sash with the word *President* dangled in a loose loop around his sausage-y center.

Atop his head (and I'm taking *quite* the liberty calling it that, since his brain wasn't primarily located there) he wore an oversized cowboy hat with two cans strapped to the side. From each of those cans ran semitransparent straws that Alice suspected would've normally run into a human's mouth—she was no stranger to the beer hat—but for anatomical reasons she wouldn't think too hard about, the straws ran down, down, down, disappearing somewhere under the tentacle jumble. Beer *catheters*? It was either brilliant or lethally foolish.

In his wake, the president left a glistening trail of jaundiced goo, which the two poncho-ed servants hurriedly sopped up with rags.

"Which one of you is the Texan?" he asked, drawing closer.

Alice raised her hand. "Howdy."

"I suspect you feel right at home here."

"Yes," she lied. "I'm Captain Alice Luck, and this is my crew." She went around, introducing them individually until she got to Aubert. "And this is the client we mentioned in the communications."

"Pleasure to meet you, Mr. President." Aubert Orleans flashed the invertebrate a toothy grin that Alice thought likely to be misinterpreted as a slight.

At least their client was bothering to put on the charm, though. And why wouldn't he? Aubert wanted a prestigious match. Maybe not with whatever the hell kind of creature this president thing was (or maybe so—no accounting for taste), but at least with whatever species the mighty queen was.

Perhaps it was because Alice had lived in a world where

the British monarchs were so old it evoked rumors of black magic cabals, but she hadn't expected the queen to look so … what was the word? Exuberant? Vivacious? Literally glowing with a golden light? Yes, that was it. Her Majesty was literally glowing.

Aubert's eyes darted greedily to her as he continued his flattery. "Your city is a shining beacon of humanity. I knew the instant we landed that I and my people were the perfect fit for your subjects."

A low rumbling issued from the president as he wobbled like a Jell-O dish in the back seat of a pick-up truck hauling ass down a country road.

Alice assumed it was laughter.

"I do not call them subjects, Mr. Orleans. I call them constituents. *She* calls them subjects." He jerked a gloved tentacle toward the queen, who remained on her throne, watching with a quiet, dispassionate expression. And, you know, glowing like a fucking light bulb.

"Have you eaten?" the president asked Alice.

"Yes, Mr. President. Your excellent attendants greeted us with tacos."

From behind him, where the two servants waited with slime-soaked towels to mop up their boss's foredooming goop, their expressions changed. They were bracing themselves.

"Tacos?" the president asked. "Plain old *tacos?*"

"No, no," Alice added hurriedly, feeling the mood in the room sour. "Not plain old tacos. Double-decker tacos! *Muy delicioso!*"

The president did a one-eighty faster than should've been physically possible and bellowed, "You fed our guest from Texas *double-decker tacos?!*" Two spurred tentacles whipped out, smacking each of the servants across the face, knocking one of their Zorro masks clean off as the man went to the ground. "These are *special* guests, you complete fools! *Triple*-decker tacos at the very least!"

He whipped back around to face his distinguished guests while both servants mopped bits of slime off their own faces where they'd been whipped.

"I would like to extend my sincerest apologies on their behalf." The president extended a tentacle toward her, and, assuming she was supposed to take it, she reached out.

Dan quickly intercepted, pushing her arm back to her side.

And that was the precise moment when it clicked for her that maybe this slimy, short-fused, spurred invertebrate with a beer catheter might not be entirely trustworthy.

She received her second sign to this effect a moment later when one of the servants' whimpering drew her attention and she realized that the skin on his face where the tentacle had made contact was not only red, but slightly smoking. "The hell?" she said, stepping past the president to attend to the injured man. "You all right, *amigo*?"

"*Es* okay. *Es* fine."

"No," she said, "you're sizzling. Maybe that's the norm for some people in this universe, but you weren't sizzling a second ago, so I reckon you're not usually a sizzler."

"Don't bother yourself with those idiots," El Presidente said. "They're replaceable, and they're grateful to be of service."

"Guard your heart," Caid whispered to Vel beside him. "Cruelty to one person is cruelty to all."

She wasn't concerned. She already had plans to guard a whole lot more of herself than just her heart if El Presidente tried anything. The moment she'd entered the room with two splatterpoots in it, she'd kept her hands by her hips, ready to draw. She'd only come up against these assholes in combat once, and she still had the raised whip scar across her stomach to prove it. Many of her compatriots had died in that battle. Lesson learned: explosives might be the only way to dispatch one of these things, but the result wasn't pretty for anyone within fifteen yards.

If El Presidente decided to lose his temper, all the blasters in Little Texas wouldn't do much. These sloppy cratersuckers healed almost as quickly as you could fire a hot laser through them.

Unless you shoved them full of explosives.

Thankfully, it wouldn't come to that. Because splatterpoots weren't intellectually complicated. Vel already had this one figured out.

"Mr. President," she said, "our captain is merely showing her Texan values. Compassion is often an overlooked one, but it's crucial, nonetheless." Was that true? She had no clue. Didn't sound right, but this wasn't about Texans; this was about slimy space trash not acid whipping their captain to oblivion.

"*Por favor*, Capitan Luck," the servant whimpered, cupping hands over the burns on his face, "I'll be fine. El Presidente is correct. It's my honor to serve him. I'm grateful to be slapped, and I should have provided you at *least* triple-decker tacos."

Unsure what else to do, Alice stepped back to join the rest of her crew. Vel shot her a look like a loaded gun, and Alice decided that defending the servant wasn't the hill she wished to die on.

"Allow me to introduce you to our lovely queen." The president undulated his way toward the thrones, and, sidestepping the goo trail that the injured servants struggled to clean with their totally saturated towels, the crew followed.

Aubert leaned toward Alice. "She's sexy. Good call. She's the perfect woman for me."

"I think … I think she's already accounted for."

"Not necessarily," Dan whispered. "The president and queen are not in a relationship. In fact, most decisions for the planet are made by the two of them battling to the death."

Alice's eyes went wide. One of these days she'd actually read the cultural brief from start to finish.

"They switch out frequently," Dan continued, "but the records show there hasn't been a major decision made in the last few planetary orbits—the equivalent to five Earth years. The gossip rags are saying it's because these two might actually *enjoy* each other's company. Quite the scandal."

Alice didn't care. "What species is he?"

"A splatterpoot."

She arched an eyebrow. "Did you make that up because you didn't want to admit you don't know?"

"No. Splatterpoots are well known throughout the universe."

"And what's she?"

"Also a splatterpoot."

"No, I mean the queen."

"I'm talking about the queen," Dan said. "She's a female splatterpoot. The splatterpoots run this world."

"But she's so…"

"Tentacle-less?" he supplied. "Yes. The females need no tentacles."

"Does anybody *need* tentacles?" Alice mused.

"Your Majesty," the president said once the crew stood

before her, "these are our most highly respected guests, DeepService Team One. They have arrived with an offer of interbreeding to help the continuation of our population."

The queen gazed upon them, her eyes narrowed. A look of harsh judgment was, it turned out, universal.

The queen looked nothing like the president. Not only were the tentacles completely absent, but she had a distinct mouth. Three of them, actually, one on each head. And upon each of those heads sat three tiaras. Below those three heads was a bearlike body, hairless but with large paws that looked like they could derail a high-speed train with a single swat. The color of her skin, or what emerged of it from beneath the frills of her dress, was anyone's guess, since the golden light she radiated was so strong.

"And who do you prepose to breed us with?" she asked, her voice deep and cavernous. "Those of Blerg VFP69?"

"No, no, no," Alice said. "But close. This guy." She thumbed at Aubert. "I mean, not him in particular. His people."

"But if you would have me, Your Highness," Aubert said, "I would be all over that."

She closed her eyes, all six of them, and bowed her heads. When she straightened again, she said, "I apologize for the interruption. I was temporarily distracted by the sensation of a supernova taking place in a neighboring galaxy."

Aubert's nostrils flared. "Oh, she *is* wife material."

"Cool your jets," Alice muttered before stepping closer to the queen. "We understand that Britannica is one of the most excellent planets in the galaxy, and—"

"THE VERY BEST." The queen erupted with a flash-bang.

Alice snapped her eyes shut and covered them with her hands until the blinding light dissipated.

"Please excuse her passion," said the president. "She loves this planet, as anyone with half a brain would. But none of you are in danger from us, least of all you, Captain Luck. Earthlings have our deepest respect. As for the rest of you, you may not be from Blerg VFP69, but you are with the Depot, and because of that, you have our promise of safety. The Depot is to be revered for all it has accomplished." The president pumped two gloves in the air as his speech became more impassioned. "Survival of the fittest, that's what they represent! A corporation with some balls, as they say! Started as a humble supply company and through hard work and determination built the empire throughout the known universe that you see today! That's what I call a can-do attitude! The American spirit! We exude that in Britannica. You can't find a place with more of it, not even on Earth!"

With each emphatic proclamation, bits of goo shot from beneath him. Vel sidestepped just in time, and it sizzled on the floor behind her.

Dan knew better than to believe the bluster of a splatterpoot. They were only safe so long as the president and queen felt like keeping them safe. But that could change in an instant. He had to tread lightly. "I've had many successful dealings with your planet on Depot business over the years, but never before have I had the honor of meeting the most revered president and most majestic queen. My mission in the past has been related to trade, but today, we come with a larger purpose, and perhaps a more noble one, as you must know. We understand that the life expectancy among the splatterpoots of Britannica has decreased significantly. I believe we can help you with—"

"Lies!" spat the president. "All lies trying to discredit me! I've heard it all before. You know how they came up with that calculation?"

Dan understood how to find the average of something, but he knew better than to answer directly.

"They take *all* the people who are born on this planet—even the beastly ones!—and then they find how old each person is when they die and use *that* number to calculate it. It's rigged, I tell you! Rigged against me! Of course it's going to be lower than ever if you count the *children* who die. They're children! Only the hardy survive into adulthood, as it should be! But when you look at the oldest on our planet, well, they're far older than the average, but no one is talking about *that*."

Caid stepped in. "It sounds like you've been mistreated."

"It's true! This guy gets it! I've been president for the last forty orbits and they've treated me so unfairly!"

"Who has?" Alice asked.

"You know who! All of them! The mathematicians and the statisticians and the scientists that run things! They are weak little people who hate me for my power! The Depot's not blameless in this," the president went on. "You know who runs it, don't you?"

"No," said Vel, "we don't. I didn't think anyone did. Do you?"

"Of course I do! You don't get to be where I am without knowing a few things they don't want you to know."

With Vel listening so intently, Alice thought it might be important to follow suit. It had never occurred to her to figure out who exactly was running the Depot. The Depot was just ... the Depot. Some boring people making boring decisions at the top. That was how everything ran. What she did know was that they paid her billions of dollars. As long as the money was hitting her account—which she had no idea how to confirm but felt okay about assuming—why worry about where it was coming from?

But this was the first time Vel appeared completely clued into the present since they'd rescued her from the Alliance, and that seemed significant.

"Maybe if you gave us a name, we could confirm for you," Vel said.

"And let them know I was onto them? No way."

"Mr. President," Dan said, "as much as you revere and mistrust the Depot, may I humbly offer that we're hardworking folks trying to make ends meet in our job. We don't care much about the big powers that be, so long as they leave us alone to live our lives how we see fit."

The president, who had been wobbling ferociously, quivered slightly less. "I have to respect that. You're only trying to do your job. If there's one thing I will always respect about the Depot, it's how many jobs they've created for the common man. That's one of the reasons the queen and I signed an order that makes it easier than ever for people to compete for entertainment jobs. Auditions are the only way to ensure the common man gets a shot at the big time. They're the only thing preserving the delicate and unstoppable force we call democracy. The day your average splatterpoot can no longer be born into absolute poverty and make his way to stardom through a series of rigorous audition processes is the day our great planet of Britannica falls to the evil forces. Not one hard-working, talented Britannican should live in poverty on this planet, and you know what? Under my reign, they don't. The poverty rate is only skyrocketing because people have stopped working hard! What happened to hard work and the talent to sing a tune that will get you to the next round of *Britannican Star Cluster*?"

"Speaking of star clusters," Alice cut in, "Aubert Orleans here is from a pretty famous one."

That stopped the president in his tracks. "You don't say."

"Yes. A *wrongly persecuted* one, too."

"You don't say!" The wobbles intensified as the president leaned in.

Alice had never thought herself a master of human psychology, and she found the idea of manipulating others to be boring, unless it was for a good cause like getting into trouble or some sort of adrenaline rush, but she didn't need to understand the fundamentals of human motivation or pull a head trip to navigate her way forward now. She had a couple uncles on her mother's side who shared similar talking points with El Presidente. She knew this game.

See? she wanted to say to the rest of her crew. *Playing it by ear works. One step at a time.*

"Yes, very wrongly persecuted. He's from Star Cluster B."

"You don't say!"

Alice dodged a flying goo ball by less than an inch. "I do, Mr. President."

Nobody spoke as his tentacles twitched thoughtfully. The jangling of spurs produced a not entirely unpleasant sound. "They're not afraid to fight it out in Star Cluster B, are they?"

Aubert grinned. "Not at all. We fought for what we believed in. The rest of our galaxy wasn't ready for that kind of rugged self-determination, and so they banded together and locked us away."

"The strong and principled are rarely understood,"

muttered the president. "Remind me, Mr. Orleans, who was behind the effort to lock Star Cluster B away?"

"It was a decision passed down by the Tri-Galactic Council."

"The Tri-Galactic Council sponsored by the Depot."

Aubert nodded casually. "That is the full brand name, yes."

Alice whipped her head toward their client. He wasn't exactly a reliable source, but he seemed to be telling the truth. Or at least believed he was.

"And here you are working with them."

Yeah, thought Alice. *Here you are working with them. With us. So principled.*

"They were the ones who reached out to my planet of Trauna," Aubert explained. "They want to make things right, apparently. They believe those of us from Star Cluster B are exactly the kind of beings this galaxy—this *universe* needs to get things back on track."

"Interesting, interesting," muttered the president. "It takes a big corporation to admit when it's wrong. What say you, my queen?"

Her Majesty's left head didn't mince words. "I don't trust anyone from Star Cluster B."

"Eh, what do you know, you absolute idiot," the president muttered. "Ignore her. She might be the queen, but she's only been it for a dozen orbits, and all three of her brains are fueled by emotion and suspicion. I've been president for forty orbits. Forty! Longest sitting president in history. I've made the best decisions, and all my enemies do is bring up the child death! As if weak, talentless children haven't always died young! My enemies hate me because they envy me."

The queen had glowed in a dangerously radioactive

capacity since the president's insult, so Dan addressed her directly. "Your Majesty, I can tell you come from hardy stock. So do the people of Trauna. We believe the Yoken would be a suitable match, if you'd give them a chance."

"Suitable?" puffed the queen from her center head. "No one is suitable for a Britannican splatterpoot! Britannica is the most glorious planet that ever was or ever will be. We have perfected the things that your planet created, Captain Luck. We have extracted their essence and amplified it to wring every last drop of glory from it. There is no better planet. And we did it all for the good of the solar system. Before the splatterpoots arrived on Britannica, the planet was a joke. We saved them, gave them jobs, a purpose for higher glory. They would die for their queen and president now, and they would do it happily. Before us, they hated death. Now they love it. They wish for it. What greater gift can you give to others? Tell me."

Alice was stumped, but she wasn't stupid. "None, Your Majesty. Clearly you and your people have ruled most intelligently here. It's almost as if no one quite measures up to the splatterpoots. You must find that tedious. Here you are working so hard and for virtually no thanks to keep the peoples of Britannica happily embracing the prospect of untimely death, and yet, are you able to do the same? Do you embrace death or dread it?"

When the queen remained silent, Alice suspected she'd finally tapped a useful vein. *'Bout damn time.* These people were giving her a headache.

"What we propose," Alice continued, "is that we do for you what you have done for your people. We want to find you a match, that leaves you begging for the warm embrace of death. And I truly believe that Aubert Orleans' people are that match."

The president wriggled onto his throne, and the servants —new ones, as the originals had scurried off and been replaced by two more with fresh towels—patted at the viscous trail.

"This intrigues me," he said. "I admit that we've been so focused on helping our people come to terms with the reality of their likely death that I've grown afraid of death myself. What a weak state in which to live! Ah, how power corrupts, I say! In this protected and lush capitol, I've lost sight of how close death is at every moment. My queen, what say you about the prospect of a possible match?"

Rather than answering directly, she said, "Is it even possible for my people to be a biological match to someone like *that*?"

While Alice was pretty sure it was meant to be an insult, Aubert puffed up his chest, interpreting it as a compliment. Fine. Whatever.

"We have run the biological simulations based upon what data we currently have on your people," Alice explained, "which is not totally comprehensive, but from what we've found so far, there is a one hundred percent chance of a healthy match. Of course, new data might slightly weaken that compatibility, but I have high hopes."

Alice didn't generally enjoy lying, but doing it in this situation, to these people, was a thrill. She wished she could do it again and then three more times.

Her Majesty tilted her heads. "And what further information would you need to certify those results?"

"A sample of egg and sperm from your people."

"Science!" bellowed the president. "You think *science* holds the answer to this?"

"Uh, yeeeah?"

"Bah! If a female of a species wants to get pregnant badly

enough, she'll do it! No science needed! If a male's juices are robust enough, he can impregnate any female he chooses! No science needed! Just like if a female doesn't want to be impregnated, her body will reject the juices! No science needed!"

"That doesn't—" Alice stopped herself.

"Have you checked the Yoken brains?" the president asked, tilting what might as well have been his head toward Aubert. "When the brains of a species get too large, it often leads to decreased sexual appetite, specifically in the females."

"No," Alice said. "I haven't"—she swallowed the rising bile—"checked the brain size."

"This is all very interesting," said the queen. "But claims of science aside, matching our species with the Yoken would be a … major decision." One of her heads snuck a glance at the president.

"Definitely. I don't expect you to consider it lightly," Alice continued.

"Consider?" The queen chuckled through two of her mouths and continued to do so as the other one said, "We don't consider things, Captain Luck. That is not our responsibility. As president and queen, our only responsibility when big decisions come along—"

"Oh no," Alice said, remembering.

"—is to each pick a side of the decision to represent and then battle to the death over it. The winner's side is the decision that is made."

"Yeah, that's not …" Alice turned to Dan, but he only cringed and tossed her a slight shrug. "Can you please give my crew and me a minute alone to chat?"

After Alice led them to the far side of the room, beneath two mounted beast heads, she pulled them into a huddle.

"Not you." She shoved Aubert out of the group. "Go flatter the queen."

Once she was free of him, she said, "Okay, so, admittedly, this thinking-only-one-step-ahead thing has us in a bit of a pinch. Dan, you said they switch out presidents and queens often, right?"

"Yes."

"So, like, it's no big deal if one of them kills the other—"

"You're not really thinking of pitting them against each other, are you?" Vel said. "You know this species match won't work even if you got both parties to agree to it. You're going to dismantle the sitting leadership of this volatile planet for a plan you know won't work out? What in the void are you doing, Captain?"

"I *thought* I made it clear that I don't know." Alice rolled her eyes. "Dan, we can let them battle to the death without, like, moral complications, right?"

"Depends on your definition of moral complications. Every time one of the pair dies, there is usually planet-wide political unrest."

"That doesn't sound good."

"It's not. They fill the vacant position in what can best described as a militia-led coup."

"They don't do, like, a talent search? I thought the president said this was a democracy."

Despite the dire situation, Dan chuckled. "Oh no, not for decades. Too many blasters around for *that* to exist."

"So, what you're telling me is that if I ask these two to make a major decision about matching with the Yoken, then it will necessarily lead to not only the death of the loser of the battle—which, frankly, I couldn't give a rat's ass about—but countless others who are too stupid to be carrying guns *or* to reestablish a democracy?"

"Yes, that's about it."

Alice pouted. This was quite the shit they'd stepped in. "They'd probably be pretty desperate for fresh genes after a bunch of their population died, though, right?"

"Captain." Vel glared at her.

"Right, right, probably not the moral thing to do. Unless …" She looked to Caid for support.

He scrunched up his nose and shook his head.

"Okay, but what if—"

"There is no 'what if,'" Vel said.

"Sheesh, fine. Do they have *anything* but black and white in that parallel universe of yours, Susy? Christ. I'm trying to get us out of this mess and get us paid."

"All due respect," Vel said, making it clear she offered only microscopic traces of respect due, "*you* got us into this mess. Perhaps the way we get out isn't the same way we got in, but by, you know, thinking more than a single step ahead."

Alice waved it off. "No. I have a better idea."

"And that is?"

"Stall. Then escape."

"Void swallow us all," Vel muttered as Alice broke the huddle.

"Your Majesty. Mr. President," Alice began, clasping her hands behind her back. "Before you make a decision, we would like a fluid sample from a male and female of your species to ensure there is even a decision to be made. We won't, like, test it with science or anything. We'll, um"—she considered what would work with her uncles in this situation—"*pray* upon it?"

"Of course!" the president replied. "Ask the mighty Blob for guidance. Such faith you have! What a true Texan."

"Would each of you be willing to provide a sample? For

the prayer. We'll give you some privacy, obviously. Not … not right here."

The president blubbered amusedly. "No need for privacy. Servant! Come here, you little Mexican."

Collectively, DeepService Team One cringed.

"Sir. Mr. President," Alice pleaded. "Not right here. I'm afraid the conditions might affect the, er, sanctity of the sample."

"Very well," said the president reluctantly. "I'll supply your sample in a quiet and holy place."

"And I as well," said the queen. "How long before you will know whether it's a match?"

Alice cleared her throat, readying herself for another delicious lie to these assholes. "As we all know, the Blob works in mysterious ways and on its own time, but hopefully no more than a few hours."

"And are you docked at Port Aransas?"

Alice looked to Vel, who confirmed with a slight bowing of her head.

"Then we will have a messenger send the samples to you."

Alice grinned. Everything was going according to her non-plan, meaning they were not dead yet. "Thank you."

"Before you return to your ship," the president said, "please, I beg of you, let one of the Mexicans serve you quadruple-decker tacos."

Feeling mighty proud of herself, and counting down the seconds until she could gloat to Vel about it, Alice bowed her head. "It would be our *honor*."

CHAPTER
ELEVEN

"The next step now is… what?" Dan said, keeping pace with his captain as they passed through the hustle and bustle of Little Texas. "We run away?"

"Pretty much," said Alice. "Unless there's a chance the two species could be a match."

"Which we already know there isn't," Vel said from her other side, "since Dan ran it by Allura."

"Ah, right."

"What was that?" Aubert poked his head between them.

"Nothing," said Alice, shoving him out of their conversation. She shot Caid a look, and the therapist took the hint and engaged the client with superficial compliments.

"That's not entirely correct," Dan added. "Technically, there's a chance, but it's a negligible one."

Alice puffed up her chest and let out a loud belch that tasted like quadruple-decker taco. "I'll let science be the judge of that."

"Don't say that word too loudly." Vel's eyes darted

around them. "You saw how they feel about— Did you already eat *both* of those?"

Alice licked the last of the grease from her fingers. "What am I supposed to do, carry quadruple-decker tacos around? I need my hands free if I'm going to play some Stand Your Ground."

"I thought we were heading back to the ship," Vel said. "You know, *to run away*."

"All in good time, Susy. Once we run away, there's no coming back, is there? Now's the time to check off all the items on our Britannica bucket list!"

"Bucket list?" asked Vel.

"Yeah, all the things you want to do before you kick the bucket. Before you die."

"I don't have one of those," Vel said, "and certainly don't have one pertaining to Britannica. If I did, there would only be one item: not bucket here."

Alice groaned. "That's not how you say it."

"I have a list," Dan chimed in, feeling much more chipper now that they were heading away from the capitol. "I heard there's a street in Little London that's entirely sooty chimneys. They break everyone into teams of chimney sweeps, and then you shoot at each other."

"Oh, like laser tag?" Alice said, ready to give Dan the order to lead them to Little London.

"Yeah, but with low-caliber blasters."

"And by low-caliber, you mean they're not lethal?"

"Depends on if you get hit in the head or not. But with the nature of popping out of chimneys, it's mostly head shots."

"I'd like to visit Little California," Caid said from behind them. "The first Multitarian Worship and Meditation Center ever was built there, and the original holographic hot springs still flows. It would scald all of you to death, obviously, but the heat would cause *me* to resonate at the same frequency as the center of this universe. I can't even imagine what that would feel like. True oneness!"

Alice wasn't impressed. "Sounds lame."

"Oh no," Dan said, his almond eyes wide. "Little California is an amazing place. I've been there. The Multitarian Center is right by the Manson Mansion, which is an adrenaline rush all its own. And remember that fungus we ate on Jaspariampt?"

"Very well and hardly at all," Alice replied truthfully.

"They have an entire field of it. You get to pick your own."

She grabbed Dan's arm, ignoring the strangeness of the smooth armor plating on her fingertips. "Oooh! Let's go there first! I bet the chimney thing would be more fun afterward!"

Vel stepped in. "We don't have time for this. If we're going to ditch, we need to get our asses back to the ship."

"We're ditching?" Aubert said, sticking his head back into the conversation.

"No." Alice shoved him out again. "You seem a little agitated, Susy. Thankfully, I know just the pizza place for us to hit."

"We don't have time for Flip the Table, Captain. I don't understand how you can—"

The sound of a blaster shot accompanied a sizzling heat that passed narrowly between Alice and Dan and put an abrupt end to the conversation.

"Shit balls!" Alice jumped back far too late to make a difference. "Which five-year-old can't be trusted with their toy?" She looked around, ready to scold.

The second shot had better aim, or worse, depending on

the intended target. Alice was pretty sure *she* had been the target, in which case, great shot.

The heat of the ray singed straight through the flesh of her left bicep, and she yowled and clutched her arm, feeling the cooked skin slide away beneath her fingers. She dropped to the ground, cursing, as the jumpsuit fabric around the hole sizzled and smoked.

Dan dropped to the ground with her and curled into an armored ball. Vel grabbed Aubert and pulled him to the ground with the rest of them.

Oh, this again, Alice's slow brain said. She'd almost forgotten that a group of someones seemed intent on murdering her and her crew.

While a few of those nearby in the crowd looked around with a lazy curiosity for the source of the blast, no panic resulted. After all, the body count was part of the fun, hence the scoreboard that kept the daily tally. When the crew had passed it on their way to the capitol, it was already up to fourteen.

"Oh void, it hurts!" Aubert cried from beneath Vel. "I'm dying! They've killed me!"

"You're fine," the lieutenant snapped. "It grazed your wrist. Shut up. *Shut up.*"

"We gotta move," Alice said. "We're too exposed. Allura."

From the earpiece: "Yes, Daddy?"

"I hate to do this to you, but we need another extraction."

"Anything you like, I'll do it."

"Great. This is all no-fly space, so they'll probably shoot at you. All of them. They'll think it's a game."

"Ooh … kinky."

Alice grinned despite herself. "You're good at being bad, Allura."

Staying low, the crew hustled through the crowd, passed between the giant sentries, and made it outside the barbed-wire fencing of Little Texas. Vel was in the lead, weaving and bobbing to make tracking them trickier for their mystery assailants. Another blast zipped over their heads, and when Aubert whimpered, Alice gladly elbowed him in the side with her good arm. "Keep moving!" Finally, they turned a corner behind a large building, and Vel led the way through a blacked-out glass door.

"Everyone okay?" Alice asked, panting and grimacing with every small movement of her blasted arm.

"No!" shouted Aubert. "Why was someone shooting at you? What'd you do to them?"

Alice held up the hand that wasn't clutching her gory bicep. "I'm gonna need you to rethink what you just asked. What's hurt?"

"What's *hurt*? My wrist! My blasted wrist!" He held it up and shook it.

"I don't see anything."

"It's— Wait, wrong one." He held up the other, and Alice was able to make out a rosy bit of flesh, possibly even a first-degree burn.

"Anyone else?" she asked.

When the others shook their heads, Alice allowed herself a moment to breathe. Her arm hurt like hell, but there were more important matters. Firstly, where were they?

Vel had a similar question. They stood in a large entryway of a building no one had bothered to vet in their scramble. Behind a desk glowing with a thin strip of blue light, a splatterpoot woman emitting her own blue light blinked back at them in shock from two of her heads. "Can I help you?"

Vel continued taking in her surroundings, and only then did she notice the coffin-like pods lining the wall, each issuing a similar cerulean light from inside.

A pod opened, and a one-legged being sat up from inside it. Vel supposed the being was fully nude, but it was always a coin toss with races she'd never seen before. "What's going on?" demanded the uniped. "I'm trying to relax."

"Oh my God," Alice said. "Is this a …"

"Tanning salon," Dan finished. "We must've crossed into Little Jersey."

"*Excuse* me," said the splatterpoot, hurrying toward them, "this is a place of worship. You either need to leave or keep your voices down."

Alice ignored the order. She never liked the whispering kind of churches anyway. She addressed her crew as loudly as she damn well pleased: "We need to figure out how to get back to the ship without getting ourselves shot."

"We've stumbled into a little luck on that, I think," Dan said. "Everything I've read about Little Jersey indicates that those out and about are much less likely to try to shoot *Emergence* when it appears overhead than those in Little Texas. They *will* try to fight it, no doubt, but as long as it stays out of arm's and tentacle's reach, the ship is unlikely to take any damage."

"Great." Alice clapped her hands together, cringed at the searing pain from her arm, and slapped a palm back over the blistering wound. "Then all we have to worry about is the Alliance trying to murder us. No biggie."

"I don't think they're trying to murder *us* this time," Vel said, her gaze not-so-subtly jumping toward Aubert.

"Him?" Alice asked. "Why would they want to— Never

mind. Dumb question. Okay, Dan, we need your armor to protect Aubert while we load up. Susy, you and I will return any fire we encounter."

Vel frowned at the captain's injury. "That's your dominant arm, Captain. You sure you can shoot?"

"You think I can only shoot with one arm? Come on, now. If that were the case, I never would've survived the great Feral Hog Attack of '09. Buck, dumbass that he is, had stepped on my wrist the night before when we were fighting over shotgun in Charlie's truck, and all but my pinkie on that hand was swollen to shit, so I—"

"All due respect," Vel said, and that was all she needed to say.

"Right, right. Remind me to tell you the rest once we're on the ship. Allura, how much longer?"

"I sense your warm bodies inside Meatball Tanning Chapel, correct?"

Confident that was the name of this place without ever seeing signage, Alice replied, "Affirmative."

"Then I'm already here. Just waiting for you to come."

Alice snickered then turned to her group. "Okay, we're going to make a run for it. Ready?"

"I don't know if I can make it," Aubert said.

Vel grabbed him by the back of the collar and shoved him toward Dan. "I'm *almost* past the point of caring, if that inspires you at all."

The crew congregated by the door as Alice took a deep breath. "On the count of three."

"If you'd like to convert," came the voice of two splatterpoot heads in unison, "we have monthly member—"

"Hell no. Three!"

They charged out of the tanning chapel as DeepCUT *Emergence* dropped down through the clouds. The sudden appearance drew the attention of those hurrying around the streets of Little Jersey, and Dan's encyclopedic knowledge was proven correct yet again. Those who noticed the ship overhead shook fists at it, hurled fighting words, and a few even jumped hopelessly skyward at it, taking swings that caught nothing but air, and shouting:

"Youse guys! Lookadat!"

"Eh, what's with this wise guy?"

"Who does this bozo think he is, flying a ship here?"

"Somebody oughta teach him a lesson!"

"You think you're a tough ship? Yeah? You a *tough ship?* Come show me!"

Alice used the leaping, gesticulating crowd to her advantage and ducked down and out of sight, leading the way toward the shadow of *Emergence,* keeping an eye out for assassins as she went.

"It seems they want to break off a piece of this," Allura crooned in Alice's ear. "There's a fire escape on the back of the nearest Flip the Table. Take it up to the roof, and I'll lower the harnesses."

"I'd love nothing more than to wear a harness for you. Lead the way."

Staying low, they continued through the busy streets of Little Jersey.

"Just a little more, Daddy. So close. To the left. So close. Almost there. Up. Higher."

Alice, now feeling breathless from more than the running, was so absorbed in Allura's instructions that she forgot why she needed the extraction to begin with.

A blast exploded the wall by Alice's feet and Aubert's head as they rushed up the narrow fire escape, reminding her. Climbing the rickety steel ladder single file meant Dan was no longer able to use his armor as protection, leaving their client a sitting duck.

Vel returned fire in the general direction of the source but still couldn't get eyes on the shooter. The brick wall exploded again in a shower of debris, and Aubert howled. Alice whirled around in time to see him collapse to the ground.

"Christ, I hate this guy." She dropped to her knees a step above him as Dan skidded to a stop to avoid a pile-up. "What's hurt?"

Aubert had slapped a hand to his face, obscuring the right side from view. "It was so close! I think I took shrapnel to the cheek. Void take me, I'm going to be ugly!"

"Good thing it's what's on the inside that counts. Oh wait." She grabbed his wrist and pulled it back to reveal …

His face. The same face as always, except with a little redness below the eye. Perhaps that was even a scratch she could see.

She cursed again and pulled him to his feet. "You fall over again, we're leaving you."

The harnesses were already waiting for them when they reached the roof, and Dan shoved Aubert into the closest one before hopping into one next to him. He hugged Aubert to him, using his armor as best he could, and said, "Allura, bring us in."

Alice could only imagine what the operating system replied in his ear.

"You two next," Alice said.

"No, you go," Vel said. "I'll provide cover."

"What sorta captain would I be then? Get your ass up." She shoved the harness at the lieutenant, whose need to comply with orders took over. Caid slipped into his holographic harness, which seemed like one big, bullshit pantomime to Alice, but she would let that annoy her later.

Zip! Up they went. Alice was the last one left on the roof. They were almost out.

Grabbing the remaining harness, she holstered her weapon for one nerve-racking moment to get her legs through the loops without accidentally shooting her own foot off. As she tightened the waist strap, she scanned the nearby buildings for any movement. Nothing.

Only when she gave the street beneath a cursory look did a familiar shape emerge from the pugnacious crowd.

A goddamn cactus.

Had it regenerated the arm she'd shot off in Vel's rescue, or was this *another* cactus?

She reached for her blaster, but the handle was stuck against a strap of the harness. She struggled with it, but it only seemed to get more tangled. "Get back, Alliance scum, or I'll blow off your limbs! Again. Or maybe for the first time, I don't know!"

The cactus didn't flinch. "We ain't your enemy, Captain Luck."

"Then stop shooting at us, you dipstick!" Finally, she slipped her weapon free, but before she could blast another arm off the guy, she paused. "Wait, you called me Captain Luck. You know I'm not a janitor?"

"Abort the mission," he called up from below. "It isn't done in good faith. It'll end in slaughter."

"Says the guy shooting at us! You got a lot of nerve, pal!"

"We ain't your enemy."

"Allura, take me—"

"Ask your lieutenant. Ask Supersymmetry Machiavelli who the real enemy is. She knows."

"*Supersymmetry*? The fuuuuuuuuuuu—" With a hard yank, she was jolted skyward.

Alice blinked, letting her eyes adjust to the dim hangar of *Emergence*. The rest of her crew was already there, and Caid buzzed around them, asking them how they felt and reminding them that trauma could be hard to spot in the moment and to be sure to take care of their hearts in the coming days.

Aubert Orleans was still moaning when Vel all but dragged him onto the elevator with the rest of the crew. He hardly had one foot on the bridge before she said, "Why don't you go have a rest, Aubert? It's been a long day, and an assassination attempt will take it out of a person."

"Why were they trying to kill me?" he asked, pressing a palm to his cheek. The wrong one, Alice noted.

"Probably because they're so jealous of you," Vel said, her voice flat as the steel side of a meat cleaver.

"Ah, yeah, that makes sense."

"Susy is right," Alice said. "Go have a lie-down. Allura can get you the bandages you need through the deposit slot."

He narrowed his eyes at her. "I'm supposed to ... bandage *myself*?"

"Yes," Alice said, unable to keep the agitation out of her voice as the adrenaline wore off and her arm started to throb in full. "It's the manliest thing I can think of. But if you'd like for Dan to come do it for you?"

"No, I'm fine. I'll... I'll be okay." He stuck his chin into the air. "I'll make it. Don't worry about me."

I'm not, thought the crew.

Alice watched him leave the bridge, then looked down at her arm. "Allura. Bandages, please. And whiskey."

"Yes, Daddy. Would you prefer bourbon, scotch, Irish—"

"Whatever you've got that'll make my throat hurt more than my arm."

She grabbed the bandages and bottle from the slot by the kitchenette and plopped down at the table. She'd never heard of Wild Harkle Whiskey, but she took a quick swig of it anyway. Spicy, sweet, and that was all she needed. It could've been antifreeze at that point and she wouldn't have cared.

The antiseptic stung like a jellyfish was humping her bicep, but at least she didn't have to hear Aubert's complaints any longer. No one said anything as the crew caught their breath.

When Caid sat across from her as she wrapped the gauze around her arm, she expected him to say something stupid, would have invited it, even, for an excuse to gripe away the pain radiating through her nerves to her spine. But he simply sat there.

It was annoyingly comforting.

Dan and Vel, meanwhile, flopped down into two of the seats facing the window. Allura had taken them up above the clouds so that one of the sunsets was visible above the horizon, the sky glowing like a bruise above it.

As Alice took another long drink from the bottle, Dan asked they question they were all thinking. "What now?"

CHAPTER
TWELVE

"What now?" really was the question of the hour.

Alice didn't know.

Vel didn't know.

Dan didn't know.

Caid knew, but no one would like his answer as it involved sitting in a circle and breathing deeply.

The harsh whiskey down her throat burned away the last of Alice's sympathy. "I say we go ahead and match them. The Britannicans and the Yoken might not be a genetic match, but odds are good they'll destroy each other before they figure that out."

Dan turned his chair away from the sunset to face his captain. "I understand why you would want the Yoken and the Britannicans to enter into mutual destruction. I don't think anyone in this room doesn't understand that. But the Britannicans don't deserve it, and I don't know enough people from Star Cluster B to condemn them either."

"No way," said Vel, "we're not pretending everyone from Cluster B isn't a nightmare. I was with you about the Britannicans, Dan, but not that."

Alice shot her the finger gun. "Supersymmetry is right."

Vel's head jerked back like she was slapped. "What did you call me?"

Alice stared her down. "That's your full name, right? Susy is short for Supersymmetry."

"Yes, but no one calls me that. Just like no one calls Dan by his full first name."

Alice looked at Dan through fresh eyes. "You're a Daniel? I can't see that for you. Dan is much better."

"Not Daniel," he said. "Danger."

"Stop."

"What?"

"That's not your name."

"It is," he said plainly. "My parents named me that."

"Oh yeah?" Alice said, incredulously. "Danger Zone? What are their names, Twilight and Construction?"

Caid placed a palm in front of Alice on the table. "I sense this is upsetting you. What emotion is at the core of this? Do you feel betrayed by the fact that you didn't know their full names?"

Alice attempted to waft his hand out of her space as Dan returned the conversation to the more important topic. "The Britannicans are idiots, sure. But don't you see how they've been made to be that way? They were once a rich and thriving culture. Then Strumpkins from Blerg VFP69 arrived, sent word back, and everything changed. Britannica, formerly Flugrasiaz'ii, was stripped of anything the rest of the universe would consider culture. Eventually, the splatterpoots were inserted into leadership, and they continued to make a mess of the place. That doesn't make every native species on Britannica deserving of being wiped out."

"And I reckon that *is* what we're talking about here, isn't it?" Alice asked. "Whoever we match the Yoken with will be wiped out. From what we know of Cluster B, that's almost inevitable." She took another swig for courage. "This mission isn't alien husbandry, at all. It's warfare."

Caid nodded sympathetically, but Dan replied, "I'm not saying that. I'm saying the Britannicans aren't the right people. Think about it. We've spent a little time with Aubert. If he's anything like the rest of the Yoken, they require a special level of patience and understanding and manipulation of their ego to cohabitate with. Do any of the Britannicans possess that level of emotional intelligence? If they do, I didn't see it. The match would turn into a shootout right away. It almost did in the throne room, remember? If we hadn't stepped in..." He didn't need to say the rest.

"All right, all right," Alice relented. "We won't intentionally have them battle it out. They're not betta fish. But I'm gonna need a few questions answered before I can make any more decisions about this. There's shit I need to know." She looked from Dan to Vel to Caid, and each shrank somewhat guiltily under her gaze. "Someone needs to spill all the beans on Star Cluster B. What the hell happened with them? The president claimed that the Depot locked them in that force field?" Dan looked the guiltiest, so she started with him. "Spill."

"Fine, I—" He looked around the bridge. "They're logging all of this. I don't know that we can ..."

Alice's eyebrows shot up. *Oh, so it's this kind of dirt.* That sure made it interesting.

"Allura," Alice said. "It's time for you to be bad. Can you give us five minutes without recording, backdating to thirty seconds ago?"

"That would be *so* naughty. You'll have to punish me when I'm finished."

"You got it."

"Recording has been disabled."

Dan rocked from one foot to the other, clearly anxious about the violation of protocol.

"You good?" Alice asked.

"This is just ... Yes, I'm fine."

"Caid? I'm declaring this a group therapy session, so you can't tell anyone jack or shit, understood?"

"I hear you."

The lieutenant didn't appear the least bit bothered by the breach of protocol. That was unusual. What ever happened to following orders? Add it to the growing list of strangeness surrounding Vel. "Okay, Dan, let's hear it."

"Now"—he held his palms out defensively—"this is only what I've heard. There's no way to confirm it. Though I did hear it from sources who have been credible in everything else."

Alice motioned impatiently for him to get on with it.

"The reason the Depot was responsible for caging in Star Cluster B was because they were the ones responsible for creating it."

"Come again?"

"Well, not the stars or planets or anything—they didn't create that—but the population that was so murderous. The Depot made them that way. That's the rumor, at least. Star Cluster B was an approved testing ground for their initial mission."

"Initial mission? For the first DeepService Team One?"

"I believe so."

Caid added, "It wasn't called that back then. It was the GeneticExcellence Squad."

Alice felt her stomach drop at the name. "Oh. Damn. Yikes." She swigged from the bottle. "Wow."

Vel tilted her head, staring closely at her captain. "You're only *now* realizing this whole thing walks the line of eugenics?"

"Matchmaking is not eugenics," Alice declared, clearly for her own psychological protection.

"It's categorized as a subset of it in the Multiversal Encyclopedia Britannica," Vel replied.

"You think I give two hoots about *anything* that comes from Britannica?" Alice grimaced as her stomach gurgled angrily. Was it the whiskey or the new understanding that she'd professionally involved herself in eugenics practices that made her stomach roil? Never a good time when that much was unclear.

She slumped at the table. "I guess it makes sense why they pay us so much, then. Hush money."

"If it makes you feel any better," Dan continued, "matchmaking is an incredibly *mild* form of eugenics. Besides, you could totally get away with that sort of thing back then, when they created GeneticExcellence Squad. Nobody cared."

Alice pressed her fingertips to her forehead. "Please stop saying the name. And how long ago are we talking?"

"In Earth years?" Dan pouted and did the quick calculations. "About a decade and a half."

Alice narrowed her eyes. "Okay, you really *couldn't* get away with eugenics in the early 2000s. People did care about it. I was there. You could get away with a lot of things —Ugg boots, bucket hats, Maroon 5—but not blatant eugenics."

"Sorry, Captain, but you're wrong," said Dan. "I've studied the records. Eugenics is an expression of supremacy, and Homo sapiens supremacy is common on Earth to this day."

"Okay, whatever. But riddle me this: you said the squad fucked around and found out about Star Cluster B only fifteen years ago. But Aubert Orleans is *more* than fifteen years old, and— Wait, he *is* older than fifteen, right?"

"Yes."

"Obviously. So how could he be a product of the Depot's experiments a decade and a half ago?"

"Because the GeneticEx— The original mission took place about three hundred years ago in Star Cluster B."

"They ... traveled back in time?" Alice had accepted a lot of new concepts since ditching that rooftop proposal and accepting Liz Windsor's job offer. But even with as many new things as she'd learned, the possibility of traveling back in time hadn't occurred to her. If it was possible, she had a whole laundry list of things to change, starting with Matt Growski at that bonfire, and ending with that time she accidentally ripped a real crowd-leveler of a fart while slow-dancing with Tucker King. She could go back in time and stop her younger self from eating four Santa Fe Gorditas from Taco Bell right before the middle school dance!

Some people never learn, she thought, remembering the quadruple-decker tacos as her belly gave a warning grumble.

"In a sense," Dan replied. "It's not time travel as you probably imagine it, though. The crew beat the speed of light between planets by traveling via space fold, like we're doing now. Space folds, depending on the size, move the timeline around at different rates. Maybe don't try to figure it out."

"Good idea," Alice replied. "Anyway, the Depot tried to make some sort of, what, weapon by screwing up everyone in Star Cluster B?"

"Not at all. Star Cluster B was long known as one of the most intelligent and shrewd places in the universe. Some of the greatest thinkers came from it. The Depot was trying to match the two smartest known populations, both of which existed on planets within the cluster. And that's all I've heard: that they were on a mission to create an ultra-intelligent race, but something went wrong. The result was the mess that is Star Cluster B."

Alice walked to the slot, muttered something to Allura, and a moment later she had a cold beer in her hand.

She'd had enough of whiskey. Time to sober up.

"Great. Now why in the *hell* did the Depot take on Aubert Orleans as a client?"

"I don't know." Dan shook his head. "I was as shocked as you were when I heard. It hasn't made sense to me this whole time, but I didn't want to mention it. The Depot doesn't like people who question its decisions."

"That's a shame," said Alice, "'cause I'm starting to question a lot about the folks we work for. Aren't y'all?"

Dan shrank into his armor plates, Vel shrugged, and Caid said, "Honestly, I'm here to help you three, whom I believe are genuinely good people. If I can be of service to you, I don't worry about who is paying me. It's never been about the money, since I don't have to eat, and I can survive without any kind of shelter. For me, it's always been about the *people*. I'm grateful to the Depot for the opportunity they've given me to work with great people."

"I'm sorry," Alice said, holding the cold bottle to her bandage and feeling both a bolt of pain and the ecstasy of relief, "but didn't the last people the Depot gave you the opportunity to help end up missing? What about that?"

"I told you, Alice, I can't speak about them."

She grunted. "What about you, Susy? I *know* you've been

hiding something behind that sexy and deadly shell of yours. I wanted to give you space to work it out, but I kinda ran out of patience for that about ten minutes ago when a heavily armed *cactus* told me to ask you what the hell is going on. Why the hell you talking to goddamn cactuses, Susy?"

"Cacti," she replied.

"Not gonna tell me, huh? Still?"

Vel bared her teeth in a smile. "I wouldn't want to give you information that might tempt you to plan more than one step ahead."

"Fuck off."

For a second, the lieutenant looked like she would crack, but then, tightening the reins on her expression, she said, "I think we should visit Star Cluster B."

Alice rolled her eyes. "Nah. Nuh-uh. You gotta be straight with me here, Susy. What the hell's going on, because that sounds *exactly* like something I would suggest, and you'd call me an idiot for it. Why do you think we should go to Star Cluster B after everything Dan just told us?"

Vel's eyes blazed. "I need you to trust me, Captain. Alice. I need you to trust that I have the best interest of this crew in mind."

Alice narrowed her eyes. "And do you consider getting us killed to be in our best interest?"

"No."

"Maimed?"

"No."

Despite herself, Alice sighed and relented. She was too tired to suspect her second-in-command of treachery. "Okay, then. I reckon I trust you. You haven't died yet. Perfect record."

Over the general broadcasting system, Allura said, "Recording restarting in ten … nine …"

Alice rubbed at her temples. "Go ahead and turn it on, Allura. Then get us on the path to Trauna. It might kill us all, but we're going to Star Cluster B."

And beneath the whiskey haze and the throbbing in her arm, Alice felt the familiar tingle of excited anticipation that accompanied every novel but reckless experience, and she couldn't fucking wait.

CHAPTER
THIRTEEN

Many astrological philosophers have speculated that dark energy is little more than universal anticipation. It is not potential energy, but potential gratification, an informational energy field in which quantum fluctuations wait, building suspense, shifting probabilities as events earlier on the arrow of time unfold. They are the building dopamine of the universe.

And then the moment arrives. All probabilities but one collapse into zero, and the victorious possibility shoots up to one hundred percent as the event comes to pass. The question is answered, the loop is closed, the dopamine is released. The anticipation energy has dissipated, usually into a cloud of disappointment, and the dark matter continues on, but not for this scenario. The event has been stamped on the arrow of time, never to be revisited, but always there.

Alice was unaware of how much dark energy surrounded *Emergence* as it hurtled closer to Star Cluster B, but she did know that her heart was racing at the thought of entering the containment zone and facing danger.

It wasn't so much that she was a danger whore, as she considered Dan to be in his best moments, but that predictable things were rarely dangerous, which meant that danger had an element of novelty and unpredictability that she appreciated. It kept things interesting so that she didn't die of boredom or have to think too hard about her past decisions.

The anticipation had kept her mind busy as she changed into a fresh jumpsuit that hadn't been shot through, cleaned up her arm with some high-grade substance Allura promised would feel *so good* (and did!), then returned to the bridge to finish sobering up in the captain's seat. Vel sat to Alice's side and Dan perched near the blaster controls. Caid had graciously placed himself at the back in the kitchenette area with Aubert, and on the large screen ahead of them, Liz Windsor's face showed the smallest crinkles of concern. "I don't understand why this is necessary," she said for the second time.

"It's become necessary for us to know more about Aubert's people if we're going to find a strong match," Alice said. "Genetically, we can do without, but behaviorally and socially, we need much more data. There's not enough in the logs." She omitted the bit about Vel's push for this obviously reckless move.

"I simply do not know that it is wise," Liz Windsor continued, the worry bringing out her fake British accent.

"Why not? We spent plenty of time with Queen Phet and the Bacc'nalis before matching them. It was the only reason we were able to be so successful in pairing them with the Jejoons. If we hadn't seen the Bacc'nalis in action, we never would've guessed that it was a matter of stress hormones and that their ideal match was the long-established antidote to stress: the marshmallow. Liz Windsor, is there something you're not telling us about Star Cluster B that would change our minds?"

The lines of concern on the woman's face smoothed instantly like someone had pulled a fitted sheet tight over a mattress. "That's not it."

"It's not like you wouldn't assign us a client whose race had no chance of a suitable match, right?"

"First of all, I don't decide which clients we accept, so none of that would be my choice—"

"Whose is it, then?"

"And secondly, the Depot would never intentionally doom one of its crews to failure."

Alice felt sensation coming back to her lips. Great. Almost sober now. "You keep saying 'the Depot.' Does the person you report to have a name?"

"The Depot has its reasons for anonymity. There are entire anti-Depot pockets of the universe that would very much like to know the particular names of those in charge, and so I cannot let that happen."

"You talking about the Alliance? 'Cause, yeah, we know. They shot at us again, by the way. And what about you? We know *your* name. How do you know *your* name won't get back to the anti-Depot folks? They could go after you."

"They could." Liz Windsor forced a grin that didn't make it to her eyes. "If you must head into Star Cluster B, then you must. But do be prepared. They're not like the rest of the universe." Her gaze jumped to the man sulking at the kitchenette because nobody cared about his boo-boos. "Not to say they're bad or defective in any way, merely that they're *unique.*"

"Do us a favor, Liz Windsor. Make sure we can get our ship back out through the containment field, would you? That's all we ask."

"Yes. Send a signal about an hour before your desired departure time, and I'll authorize *Emergence* to leave. Make absolutely sure that no one follows you out."

How they were supposed to make sure of that, Alice didn't know. Shoot any ship that tried? Would the Depot have their backs if they did that? Not like she wanted to shoot anyone, but she was already feeling iffy about entering the containment field of Star Cluster B, and Liz Windsor's reticence only left her feeling twitchier.

"Oh! And before I go," continued the liaison, "our base records indicate that there were, well, no records from your ship for a matter of roughly five-and-a-half minutes. No audio, visual, or mechanical or biometric data at all. Everything okay?"

"Old ship," said Vel. "Old operating system."

"Ah, right. I don't mean to lecture, but you really should have accepted the *Constant* when I offered. Next mission, then?"

Alice opened her mouth to say no deal, but Vel spoke first. "Absolutely. We would love that."

They ended the communication, and Alice could once again see clearly through the front window of the ship. From a distance, she'd been able to distinguish a distinct star cluster, but up this close, it looked like any other part of the universe to her. How had the Depot decided what to contain? What made this corner of this galaxy so dangerous it had to be quarantined? Could it *really* have been a Depot mission gone wrong? How could that have resulted in so much trouble?

Her mind jumped back to their first mission. They'd matched the Bacc'nalis with the Jejoons, and it was almost a perfect match. Almost. A Bacc'nali female and a Jejoon male were perfection, but when the sexes were switched in the pairing ... every so often something terrible and misshapen was likely to result. At least, that was what the simulation had come back with. But the time crunch had forced them to make the match anyway.

It seemed like such an innocent margin of error. Humans reproducing with other humans had similar misfires in offspring DNA. Evolution depended on small abnormalities and adaptations. But could her little margin of error, over time, amount to something that required the Bacc'nalis and Jejoons to be stuck behind a Depot containment wall?

"Entering the containment field," Allura said, "in five ... four ..."

Alice glanced around to check on her crew. Dan stared at her, presumably for reassurance. It was the least she could give him before dragging him into this bad idea, so she shot him two thumbs up and tried not to cringe when she flexed her singed bicep. Once Dan looked away, Alice turned to her second-in-command for a little reassurance herself.

Vel's face was set with determination as she stared through the window, making full use of the armrests, but somehow not gripping them. She showed no signs of fear, only a stony determination. Or maybe resignation. The two could look so much alike.

"... two ... one." A slight jolt went along with Allura's announcement, and Alice felt suddenly lightheaded. Her first thought was *Maybe I'm the one who should be sorry*. She had no idea what about, though.

"Penetration achieved," Allura announced. "We're inside."

A flashing light at the front of the bridge pulled Alice's attention. The onboard clock, which had ticked steady and reliably so far, counting ship time, was now bouncing around. "Allura. Why is the clock malfunctioning?"

But it was Aubert who answered. "It does that sometimes around here. You'll get used to it."

"I hope not."

"I've heard of this phenomenon," Dan said, "but never at this large a scale. It's usually a single cave within a planet or, at worst, the planet itself."

"Okay, but what is it?" Alice demanded.

"As we move along the arrow of time, new information is created. We call that 'history.' Theoretically, history can't be erased, but it can become scrambled."

"Please, Dan. Like I'm stupid."

"Yes, Captain. History is being collectively rewritten. If it happens frequently enough, it essentially makes the arrow of time zigzag."

"History is being collectively rewritten. If it happens frequently enough—"

Alice's eye twitched. "You already said that, Dan."

"I don't believe I did."

"Yes. You said the same thing twice. Just now."

Dan's expression turned grave. "I'm starting to better understand the containment field."

The ship lurched as a thunderous sound filled the bridge.

Before Alice could ask what had happened, Allura answered. "We have sustained a nonconsensual hit from a nearby craft."

Dan was already on it. He'd suspected something this terrible would happen the moment they entered the cluster. Usually, his anxieties never came to pass, but this time they had.

And he was ready.

He grabbed the headset off the control board next to him and slid it on. The 360 view of space around *Emergence* brought no good news. "I count eight craft within range, and more incoming. The time instability is causing most of their shots to miss, but we won't stay lucky forever. Should I return fire, Captain?"

"Yes! Duh! Shoot 'em!"

Alice stood behind her chair, gripping the back for balance in case another shot found them.

Her mind leapt to the escape pods down below. *No, you can't bail out. You're the captain!*

"Aubert," she said, "any clue what this is about?"

The Yoken shook his head, mouth hanging open. "No idea. What'd you do to piss them off?"

"What did *I* do? Nothing! We're a Depot ship. We're allowed to be here." The ship lurched again. Another bomb blast.

"You must've done *something*," Aubert insisted. "Why would they shoot at you if you were innocent?"

"They're shooting at you too, you asswipe. Get up here."

She dragged him by the shirt collar toward the front of the bridge, gritting her teeth against the pain in her arm. "Allura, can you connect us to one of the other ships?"

A moment later, a grouchy but handsome face, not unlike Aubert's, appeared in front of them.

"This is Captain Alice Luck," she said. "One of your own is onboard our ship as a guest. We come from the Depot and have permission to be within the containment zone. Please *stop shooting at us.*"

"I don't trust you," came the man's reply.

"You don't trust *us*?"

"You're firing at us."

"Because you fired at us first!"

"That's not how I remember it."

Alice shoved Aubert in front of her so that he was more

visible through the comms, then hissed in his ear, "Get them to stop shooting at us, *now*."

Aubert sprang into action. "My good man. I'm one of yours. I don't know what Captain Luck did to offend you, but I'm sure you have just cause for trying to murder her and her crew. But please, I ask for my own sake that you show mercy and refrain from pursuing us. And if you could call off the others, that would be wonderful. Don't do it for her. Do it for me."

"I don't trust you either," came the reply. And then the screen shut off and the ship lurched again.

Aubert stared expressionlessly. Then he blinked. "Your comms must be busted. Happens on these DeepCUTs. Old model. And your operating system is horrendously out of date. He clearly couldn't hear me or see my face to know I was one of his own. If he had, I'm sure he would've called off the attack right away."

"Allura," Alice shouted as an enemy ship zipped in front of them, "we need to skidoo. Find the nearest time fold and get us the hell out of here!"

"Impossible, Daddy. There is no access to time folds within the containment zone. We would have to exit the area first."

Liz Windsor said she'd need an hour's notice to get them out. No go on that, then. "Susy, take the ship controls. Let's put that war experience of yours to use. Allura, allow for manual override on navigation."

Vel's steely expression lit up, and she jumped into action, sliding into the driver's seat, slipping on her 360 headset, and taking over where Allura left off.

"This would be a lot easier without gravity in the ship," Vel said.

"Fine, whatever you need."

"Buckle up, everyone."

Alice had hardly gotten her seatbelt secured across her lap when Vel released the gravitational mechanism and everything became quite womblike.

Aubert wasn't even close to finding a place to secure himself, and he yelped as his feet left the ground and he began floating around and into things.

Nobody cared.

While Alice went along for the ride, trying desperately to focus on a single star ahead of them so as not to throw up all her poor eating and drinking decisions of the day, Vel's driver's chair had become a gyroscope, the ship rotating around her as it spun and twirled, keeping her oriented toward their destination of Trauna the whole time.

Emergence took another hit. Aubert's head bumped kitchenette cabinet.

Still, nobody cared.

"I've knocked out four of their ships," Dan said from his gunner's seat, "but there have to be forty more!"

"Keep firing," Alice instructed him.

"Allura," Vel called out.

"Yes, Big Susy?"

"Don't— Whatever. You hanging in there?"

"I feel slightly dizzy. What time is it?"

Alice's eyes jumped back to the skipping clock.

"Allura," Vel said, "can you home in on Trauna again? I took my eye off it for one second and I want to be sure we're heading for the right place."

"Yes, Daddy."

"Wrong person," Alice said, feeling genuine panic yawning and stretching somewhere in her mind. "*I'm* Daddy. She's Big Susy."

This was obviously bad. Their onboard operating system

was out of sorts, and they were trapped in this star clusterfuck for at least another hour. Would they be safe once they landed?

Alice seriously suspected not.

"Coordinates missing for S-S-S-S-S-SC-B Trauna."

A tiny bell rang in Alice's head, but it was blasted apart by another hard lurch. A hollow sound echoed up from the cargo hangar below, and the possibility that they might make it all the way to Trauna only to be stuck there occurred to the captain for the first time.

"Come on, Allura! We're not losing you. Hang in there. You'll have a minute to rest once we've touched down. Hang in there, my sexy warrior."

"Yes, D-D-D-Da— D-D-D—"

"Shh, save your strength."

"Singularity swallow us!" Vel cursed. "There are even more of them coming from both sides."

"Estimated touchdown?" Dan asked.

"Ninety seconds, whatever *that* means when the arrow of time has the blasted quantum jitters!"

Speaking of which, a massive ray narrowly missed the nose of the ship, and Dan began shaking.

"Fuck me sideways." Alice unclipped her seatbelt and pushed herself toward the minister in the gunner's seat. Not wanting to unbuckle him while he was in such a state, she took the headset from him and sat on his lap, locking her feet behind his ankles, grabbing the weapons controls to anchor herself, and pretending he was a massage chair instead of a crucial member of her crew in a fit of jitters. She imagined the ship nearest to them had a flat, round snout and two glassy demon eyes, and then she began firing.

Dopamine flooded her brain when she struck the first fatal hit that sent a small ship bursting apart into space debris. "Sooooooie, motherfuckers!" The 360 view stopped being so disorienting after a few more seconds, and it was game on.

By happy accident, she found a spot on a particular model of craft, of which there were now dozens swarming them like flies, that would make the enemy's ship explode instantly if hit. By happier accident, she realized she could hold the control sticks in such a way that firing *Emergence's* mega gun felt like simply pulling the trigger of her favorite hunting rifle. And no reloading necessary here.

"Susy, we close?"

"Thirty more seconds, Captain."

When a ship twice the size of theirs appeared out of nowhere, Alice cursed a blue streak and began firing. Nothing seemed to touch it, though. "We got a problem."

"I see it, Captain."

Vel had, in fact, noted it long before Alice pointed it out. She'd seen the gravitational bend around the object on her control panel. Not much, but enough for the sensors to know something was there, veiled though it was.

The lieutenant checked the levels. The ship was using far more energy than it was getting back from the surrounding cosmic rays and radiation. *Emergence* could travel indefinitely at normal speeds, even with a handful of time-fold jumps in there, but once manual override was engaged, the balance became lopsided. If the energy reserves became entirely depleted, they would be done for, floating with whatever momentum they had but unable to adjust their course with any swiftness. If that happened, Vel had no doubt they would be swallowed whole by the incoming giant of a ship —if they weren't shot to oblivion first.

They had to get out of there. Maybe one last surge would be enough. It would have to work, and she would have to wait for precisely the right time so it would carry them the rest of the way to Trauna with enough fuel left to orbit to their desired location …

"Captain, we're running low on energy, but I believe we have enough for one—"

"Do it! Whatever it is!"

Maybe having an inexperienced captain *wasn't* bad all the time.

Vel locked on to Trauna, aligned their trajectory for maximum energy efficiency, and then hit it. *Emergence* shot forward, and the stars gained tracer tails as the planet of Trauna ballooned in size. As long as they could keep this a straight shot and nothing moved in front of them, they were gold.

Something moved in front of them.

Vel thought it was a ship, but it could have been an asteroid or one of the many pieces of the space junk that circulated every civilized planet.

She dodged it in time, but with the speed at which they were going, the juke had taken them largely off course. She adjusted quick as she could. "Cease fire, Captain. We can't spare the energy now."

Reluctantly, Alice removed her fingers from the triggers. "Susy, we gonna make it?"

Vel ran the calculations over and over in her head, scanning the charts that hovered in front of her eyes beneath her helmet. "I believe we'll make it *somewhere*. Are they still on our tail?"

"No, that plan of yours shook them. They'll be after us soon if we slow down, though."

The planet of Trauna nearly occupied their complete field of vision through the front window as the energy indicator of DeepCUT *Emergence* went from red to black. Vel slumped slightly in her seat as the ship continued to hurtle toward the planet on momentum alone. Without any energy left, they would land wherever they landed. A controlled orbit to the desired location was now out of the question.

Aubert whimpered as he floated near the elevator, muttering something to himself about assault and battery and suing. Though Caid was trying to talk the man down, figuratively, he was having little success.

As Alice heaved an exhausted sigh, it occurred to her that her massage chair had stopped. "You okay, man?" she asked over her shoulder.

"Fine," came Dan's weak reply.

She pushed herself off his lap. "Can we get the gravity back on?"

Vel slipped off her helmet. "Nope."

"Are we going to crash-land?"

That question required a more verbose answer. "I suspect the cosmic radiation in the cluster will manage to charge us enough that I can pull back once we enter the planet's atmosphere. But we can't do anything else in the meantime. Keep the oxygen on and wait."

"How long?"

"Twenty seconds. You might want to get yourself secured."

Aubert clearly wasn't listening, so Alice launched herself over to him, grabbed him under the armpits, and kicked off the wall in the direction of a spare seat. She buckled him in, told him to be a good boy for Mommy if he wanted a dipped cone later, and then got herself secured in her captain's chair.

Flames blazed at the edges of the windshield as they passed through the hazy outer layer of the atmosphere through fine clouds of dust, until the world opened up below them. Not *far* below them, though.

Vel had her headset back on, muttering to herself, "Hold steady, Machiavelli ... not yet ... not yet ..." Then she pulled hard on a lever, and Alice felt like her stomach might pop out of her mouth as the seat restraints pressed into her soft bits.

The ship thrust backward against its own momentum, and a sound like the whoosh of a flamethrower engulfed the bridge.

Emergence went down hard, skipping like a rock after the initial impact until a mighty jolt signaled the end of the landing.

Rubbing at her neck, Alice wondered if chiropractic treatment for whiplash was covered by Depot benefits.

Either way, it was nice to be somewhere solid.

Gravity was back, and she was grateful for it, even as it made her feel very, very fat.

"Allura," Alice said. "You there?"

In the softest whisper: "Yes, Daddy."

The captain exhaled deeply. "It looks to be pretty sunny out there—that's a good sign, right?"

Vel confirmed with a nod. "Landing on the daytime side was fortunate. Assuming there's no profound structural damage, *Emergence* can recharge in the rays. Should be ready to escape the orbit in perhaps six to eight hours."

"*Is* that lucky?" Alice mused. "I guess we'll have to see how hospitable this planet is."

"I can't wait to show you all of it," Aubert said, dropping all his complaints of injury and threats of a lawsuit. "You'll love my people. The best in the entire cluster, and that's a guarantee. Well, not François. He's lazy and conniving. And not Lorraine, either. God, what a bitch. Nicole is a real cunt, too …"

Aubert was still rattling off his list of his most hated Yoken, which might've extended to the whole population if they'd had more time, as the crew readied themselves in the hangar.

Alice slid up to Dan, extending him a booster.

He looked down at it with surprise. "You don't need it?"

"Nah. If I start getting sleepy, I'll do something reckless to get my heart rate back up. Come on, you need it after those jitters."

Dan swallowed the tablet gratefully then spoke to the crew. "There's very little known about Trauna or any of the other planets within Star Cluster B. What is known is vastly outdated. However, if the jumping clock told us anything, I think we can expect strange things to happen. The best known survival technique for these sort of time-space abnormalities is to not get too attached to your perceptions as reality. At the same time, do not let anyone make you doubt your reality. Otherwise—"

"Come on, you square," Aubert said, sauntering to stand next to the minister of weapons and culture. "This place is great. You won't have a problem with it at all. Best planet in the system, if not the galaxy. You're getting them all worked up over nothing." He addressed the others, who wished he wouldn't. "Listen, these guys are great. You're going to enjoy yourself, and Emperor Best is the MAN! He's got this sweet palace, and everybody loves him. Great guy." He paused. "I mean, he can be a dickhead sometimes. And he's one ugly motherfucker, truth be told." Aubert chuckled then waved it off. "Anyway, you'll meet him for yourself. You're gonna love him." Strutting toward the port, he held out his arms. "Welcome to my wonderful home!"

"I hope he's killed *right* away," Vel muttered, pulling the leg of her jumpsuit down over her ankle blaster.

"Wouldn't that sort of jeopardize our mission?" Alice asked.

"I'm *so* close to being past the point of caring."

As they stepped out onto the planet, the throbbing in her arm returning as the adrenaline of the crash landing dissipated, Alice took in the strange, arid landscape. The world around her was rust and ink blots, and what scrub brush had managed to exist scurried around like its roots were on fire. And it screamed a little.

But most importantly, as far as her vision stretched, there was no sign of civilization. Normally, such a thing following a crash landing would be one hundred percent a bad thing. But considering the star cluster they were in, a part of Alice was also relieved.

Eventually, though, they would need to track down inhabitants who weren't shrieking shrubs. And some water. They could only carry so much of it with them, and whatever star was central to this system shone like it had something to prove.

"Any idea where we are?" she asked their unofficial and unqualified guide.

Aubert looked around. "Oh, I think we're close to something."

Unhelpful. "Okay, then please lead the way to … something."

Vel pointed toward a craggy peak. "Why don't we start there? Get a better view."

"Great thinking." Unfortunately, the craggy peak was easily three miles off over dusty and uncertain terrain. Was quicksand a thing here, Alice wondered? Seemed like the kind of place to pull shit like that.

She had never encountered quicksand in her life, though she, like most Earthlings, had thought often of its dangers as a child. But neurotically fixating on a danger is not the same as educating oneself about the danger, and she never learned how to properly identify or avoid the trap. All she knew was not to try to get oneself out once one was in it. But if they were *all* in it …

Aubert kicked one of the scampering bushes, and it squealed as it flew through the air. "Don't worry," he said, turning back to the group, "they like it when you do that."

"It doesn't hurt them?" Dan asked.

"It does. Causes internal bleeding that eventually kills them, too, but they enjoy it all the same. Guess they want to die."

Dan scanned the horizons, a lip curling at the ruddy view. "Fair enough."

As the peak slowly drew closer, the rustiness was interrupted by more and more of the ink blots—bumps on the ground so dark they swallowed the light entirely, making the dimensions of them hard to gauge. Alice attempted to step over one, misjudged, and caught the toe of her Texas flag boot on it, stumbling forward and cursing.

Vel arched an eyebrow. "Don't be such a clumsy idiot."

Alice glared at her. "Excuse me? You don't get to talk to me that way."

Vel jerked her head back. "Talk to you what way?"

"Calling me a clumsy idiot!"

Vel arched a brow at her captain. "What? I never called you that."

"You just did! Not even five seconds ago."

"What the void are you talking about?" Vel looked to Dan. "Did you hear me call her a clumsy idiot?"

Dan shrugged. "No, I didn't hear anything like that."

"Me neither," added Caid.

Alice's mouth fell open. "The *hell*?"

The landscape transitioned further, adding more and more jet-black underfoot and slowing their progress, especially that of the captain, who was starting to believe her own brain had called her a clumsy idiot, and if one's brain was to the point of cooking up imagined exterior criticism, things must have gotten pretty bad.

Dan was the next to trip, and not in any subtle way. He flew forward, hands out to catch himself before he remembered what he was and curled into a tight, armored ball. He bounced around between rocks until finally coming to a stop. When he opened up, he got to his feet and continued walking as if nothing had happened.

"You okay?" Vel asked.

Dan looked at her strangely. "Who, me?"

"Yes, you. The one who just rolled all around into sharp rocks. Are you okay?"

Dan scoffed. "That never happened."

Vel stopped walking. "It did. Just now. You only got to your feet five seconds ago."

He cast her a worried glance. "I think the heat's getting to you."

"Yeah," Alice said, looking the lieutenant up and down. "Are you okay, Susy? That's an insane thing to think you saw when it didn't happen."

Vel's eyes shot open. "I— Wait. You're screwing with me."

"Strange conclusion to jump straight to," Caid said. "A little paranoid. If you need to talk about what's really bothering you instead of making up scenarios about Dan, you know my door is always open."

"What in the blasted quasar?" Vel cursed, her hand hovering instinctively near the weapon on her hip.

"Wait!"

All eyes turned to Aubert.

"Ah, I see what's happening here. See this?" He bent down and grabbed a loose piece of the inky stone. "It's the ghasselite. It causes things like this. Someone claims something happened, and everyone else swears it didn't."

Alice felt relief wash over her. She'd been right about what Vel said. It wasn't just her imagination. She wasn't losing her mind!

Aubert hurled the rock at another wandering bit of scrub but missed by a few feet.

"I don't follow how that relates to everyone saying Dan *didn't* fall and curl into a pinball," Vel said.

"Ghasselite creates an unsteady reality."

"So, what I saw happen to Dan ..."

"Never happened."

"Hold on," Vel said, "that's not what I was saying. It *definitely* happened."

"No, it didn't."

"I saw it."

"You couldn't have."

Vel's fingertips touched her blaster. "I did!"

"And you," Alice said, pointing at her lieutenant, "definitely called me a clumsy idiot!"

"No, I didn't."

"Yes, you did!"

"No, she didn't!" Aubert, Dan, and Caid said together.

Aubert rolled his eyes. "Women, am I right? Always

making things up." He kicked another shrub, which yelped, then he started again toward the peak.

Alice stood beside Aubert at the edge of a large overhang that was the highest point around. She was sure to keep out of arm's reach from him in case he got the urge to push her, which seemed likely for an asshole like him.

Vel's suggestion had been sound, as this vantage point gave them a much better view of Trauna. Alice could see for miles and miles. The horizon on this planet seemed twice as far away as any she'd seen on Earth, and in all the area surrounding them, not a single trace of a city could be found.

"Guess we're screwed." She stopped shielding her eyes from the sun, letting her hand fall to her side as she turned to face her crew. "A whole lot of nothin'. If we can't get *Emergence* back up and running, I'm afraid we're all going to die."

"Hold on," Dan said, stepping forward, closer to the edge. "Right there! Not two miles off! It's a whole city, by the looks of it!"

The rest of the crew moved closer to see where he was pointing. "There," he insisted. "The big, colorful tents, like a bazaar. They stretch for miles. Don't you see it?"

Alice shared a concerned look with Vel. "There's nothing there, Dan."

"Void swallow me," he said exasperatedly. "I see it with my own eyes. How can you not see it? We're practically on top of it."

"He's losing it," Aubert said to Caid. "Maybe you'd better take him back to the ship and therapy him."

Dan threw his arms into the air. "Come *on*! Don't your eyes work?"

The crew, who didn't realize that the core of the overhang on which they stood was pure ghasselite, was so preoccupied with their dispute that they didn't notice the approaching figures until the group was right on them.

"Halt!"

Three strangers rode atop strange six-legged beasts whose legs shook as if they were on the downside of an adrenaline rush. The beasts' heads were mostly a pair of wet eyeballs and, below them, a tongue that whipped around and occasionally licked said eyeballs.

The beasts could have passed as overturned ripe pears, light green in color and probably pretty juicy if you cut one open.

The only thing remarkable about the riders was that they looked human.

There is truly no reason for anyone to look human. Not even humans. It is a tragically flawed evolutionary design, about as bad as they come, and that it might occur in evolution not once, but *twice* defied the odds.

Or perhaps, Alice thought, *they've come from Earth.* Had her planet transported people all the way out to Star Cluster B to populate the planets? It would explain how Aubert looked so humanlike instead of, well, literally anything else. She hadn't been on the job long, but already she'd gleaned that most sentient beings looked like something an exterminator should be dealing with.

Aubert stepped toward the strangers. "My good friends! You've found us!"

"Found you?" said the stranger at the head of the trio. "We weren't looking for you. We don't know who in the darkness you are."

"Don't know me? Ross! Come on! It's me, Aubert!"

"Never seen you in my life," said Ross.

"We went to school together! Our mothers are sisters!"

"Not a day in my life. I haven't seen you a day in my life."

Aubert then spoke to the stranger on Ross's left. "Baruggio! Come on, surely you remember me."

Baruggio shook his head slowly. "I wish I could say I did, but when I look at your face … nothing. No recollection."

"Baruggio! It's me, Aubert! Aubert Orleans! We grew up next door to each other. I murdered your sister in front of you! You picked me out of a lineup! You testified against me in the trial!"

"What a strange thing to lie about," Baruggio remarked.

Alice shouldered Aubert aside before she had any more of his criminal past thrust upon her. "We're trying to find the nearest town. We need to speak to the emperor as soon as we can. Can you help us?"

"No town around here for miles," said Ross. "But you look like excrement. Come with us and we'll get you fed and washed up."

"We won't," explained Baruggio. "Our wives will. That's what they're there for anyway."

"Well, that," Ross added, "and the, ya know."

"Right."

"The supernovas."

"Right."

With few options left, and with Dan still claiming the city they were looking for was *in front of them*, the crew of DeepService Team One followed the three strangers back to their home to be tended to by their wives.

CHAPTER
FOURTEEN

The third stranger's name was Romelda, and while Alice knew that females could have wives like males could, she wondered how this female had herself escaped what seemed like the pretty dreary fate of being made one. Perhaps it was a matter of wife-or-be-wifed in this wild universe.

The three strangers—Ross, Bargugio, and Romelda, who were not actually strangers to Aubert and becoming more and more familiar to the crew by the second—shared a home along with their respective wives.

It wasn't a home so much as a cave. But Caid had innocently referred to it as a cave while they stood outside, and everyone had told him he clearly didn't know what a cave was if he thought this was one. Nobody had seen anything less like a cave in their lives.

Once they were inside the cave, though, deep underground and away from the ghasselite that stayed mostly near the surface of the planet, Dan began to think maybe Caid had been right, and this was a little like a cave.

For one, there were stalactites. That was usually a giveaway.

The tunnel opened up to a cavern that didn't deserve to be called "cavernous," since it was rather small to house all the current occupants comfortably. In the middle of it ran a stone table with three lanterns down the center. Baruggio motioned for the guests to take a seat.

Ross's wife approached Dan and set a large bowl of cold soup in front of him. "Mostly guts from the pricklecrits. The trick is to let it sit out at room temperature for three days until the bacteria really takes off, then you boil it. Kills the bacteria, but you still got all those little bacteria bodies floating around. Then you freeze it for twenty days, and it's ready to serve."

Dan looked down at the surface of the liquid where the lamplight glistened off it. Lumps and bumps of something a ghastly, pale pink bobbed in the bowl.

"Mmm …" he said. That single sound is a diplomat's go-to when someone sets something in front of them that they are expected to eat but that makes them want to retch. It was the most important tip Dan had learned in his job training and had served him well over the years.

"Take a try, then." The wife hovered so close to him, he wasn't sure if he could get the spoon to his lips without asking her to move. Swallowing hard against the rising acid in his throat, he checked that he had enough of the sweet ale they'd provided in case he needed to wash down the taste, and definitely to kill whatever microbes survived the preparation process. And then he ladled himself a sip.

Before it could touch his lips, he made the mistake of inhaling—a survival instinct universal to all those with a sense of smell about to try some new substance.

Something seemed off. A small voice in his brain told him he would die if he ate it. He tasted the soup anyway, allowing a single droplet in and hoping that alone wasn't enough to kill him.

The broth was both sour like turned milk and sickly sweet like an overripe fig. The smell reminded him of the time he found himself knee-deep in Gambuulinq shit while seed hunting with a client during his private-sector diplomacy days.

"Mmm …" he said again, his hand shaking.

"You like it?" asked the wife.

"Mmm …"

"Hot damn!" Alice exclaimed from the other side of the table. Dan looked up. She was shoveling the soup into her mouth as fast as she could, slurping shamelessly. "This is like the menudo we used to get at Jorge's Cantina after a night of heavy drinking." She sucked down another spoonful.

Beside her, a wife hovered. "You like it?" she asked, staring greedily at the captain.

"Oh yeah! This is great."

"I was worried you wouldn't like it."

"No, I love it. Really hits the spot."

"Are you sure? Because if you don't like it, I can get you something else."

"Please, this is amazing!"

The wife's face twisted into a mask of agony as she threw her hands into the air. "She hates it. She's lying to be kind."

"Huh?" Alice took a break from the soup to look around. "I'm not lying. It's great."

"It's fine," said the wife. "You don't have to like it."

Alice's spoon hovered over the surface of the soup as she looked from the wife to Dan. "Am I missing something?" she whispered.

The miserable wife shuffled to a dark corner and began to whimper. "She hates it. I worked so hard, and she hates it."

"No, no! I—"

But Dan placed a hand on her arm. "Stop feeding her praise. It's not working. Just enjoy your food." Then he added under his breath, "*Someone* should."

It wasn't just Alice who'd managed to enjoy the meal. Aubert had been treating himself generously to it as well.

The third wife set upon him. "Do you like it?"

"Yeah, now scram. I'm eating."

She gasped and scurried off to mutter with the wife who'd bothered Alice.

Vel watched the conflict with fascination but would blast this whole place to hell before she put a substance that smelled so rancid into her mouth. She hadn't survived this long, through so many precarious situations and with so many enemies, by ignoring her body's basic survival instincts. So, while the wives busily caused their scene, she sneakily poured the rest of her serving into Alice's bowl.

That only caused more problems for the crew, though, because when the whimpering wife finally self-soothed enough and returned to Alice, she found the bowl fuller than before. "You hate it! I knew it! You know what?" She snatched the dish away from the captain and carried it over to a bucket, where she dumped it.

His stomach fomenting rebellion from the single drop he'd ingested, Dan wondered how he could earn the same level of service.

The defiant act of dumping the soup set off the other two wives, who began their own laments. "They hate it! We worked so hard, and for what?"

"I already told you I liked it!" Alice protested. "Aubert likes it, too!"

"It's *okay*," he said, slurping more down.

For the duration of the meal, Ross, Baruggio, and Romelda had reclined in stuffed chairs by a small fireplace, ignoring the conflict. But now, Ross strained himself enough to stand and approach the table. "Okay, *who* upset the wives?"

Dan could feel his captain's eyes on him, begging, but he had nothing for her. He might be from the Ministry of Culture (and Weapons), but this behavior made little sense even to him.

"I told her the soup was great," Alice said, holding up her hands innocently.

Ross eyed her. "You told her it was *great?*"

"Yes!"

"Not *fantastic*? Not *the best you've ever had or ever will have*? Not *out of this world?*"

Alice blinked. "Was that what I was supposed to say?"

"Only if you meant it."

"I—"

But of course Alice wouldn't mean that. Yes, it reminded her of the menudo she used to enjoy so much, but even the best menudo had a certain deplorableness to it, a sort of self-loathing in every spoonful. That was, after all, the appeal. And while this reminded her of menudo, and she'd been exceptionally hungry, she wouldn't have called the slop fantastic.

And that left her in a bit of a pickle, one that Vel sorted out for her.

The lieutenant stood. "Let's get out of here."

It was as good a plan as any, and Alice nodded for Dan,

Aubert, and Caid, who'd been spared trouble through his inability to consume liquids, to follow.

One of the wives rushed forward. "Where are you going?"

Vel was the one to answer. "Away. We thank you for your hospitality."

"You're not *really* grateful," the wife snapped.

Alice grunted. "We *are* grateful. Y'all pulled us out of the sun and gave us some food and drink."

"If you were grateful, you would have finished your soup."

Throwing her hands into the air, she yelled, "I *tried*! Your homegirl took it right out from under me!"

Vel grabbed her. "You're playing a game you can't win."

The crew was only a few yards out into the sunlight again when the cacophony started up behind them.

"Come back!"

"Why are you leaving us?"

"Did we not do enough for you?"

"We'll be better, we promise!"

"We'll give you whatever you want!"

As the calls faded out and the red expanse stretched around them, Caid said, "That was ... a lot. Whenever we have a calm minute, we should consider talking about— Oh look!" They'd emerged from behind a large, rusty rock, and there, spreading out in all directions, was a massive marketplace of colorful tents.

Dan's eyes went wide. "That's it! I *told* you all it was there. You didn't believe me!"

"You never said anything about that," Vel replied.

"Yeah," Alice seconded. "I think I would remember if you'd pointed out the *exact* kind of place we were looking for."

CHAPTER
FIFTEEN

The colorful market surrounded the one place DeepService Team One needed to visit: the palace. If Aubert Orleans wasn't completely full of shit from the start, which was a possibility in everyone's mind, they'd found themselves on his home planet, and the one person they needed to speak with to better understand the reproductive woes of the Yoken was Emperor Best. And Emperor Best could be found, as you and anyone else could guess, in the palace.

As they drew closer to the market, a single tall spire jutted from the center of the tent expanse like a rusty nail. Made from the same ruddy material of the landscape, the structure bolted into the sky hundreds of feet and was covered in elaborate carvings that probably depicted something epic, though time had worn down the definition substantially, and all Alice could make out were a smattering of anguished faces staring out over the city.

As they approached the perimeter of the market, a gaggle of beings accosted them. "Gaggle" was the term that came to Alice's mind because a handful of the beings appeared incredibly gooselike, but, you know, if geese had scabby spikes around their necks and wore pants.

"Necklaces! You like? Palace necklaces for the pretty ladies?"

"Jesus," said Alice, sidestepping them. "All tourist traps are the same, huh?"

A goose tried to slip one of the beaded monstrosities over Vel's neck, and she swept his webbed feet out from under him with a dangerously quick kick. He fell onto his backside with a shocked honk, and the crew made their way into the bazaar.

"What do I have to do to see you in a new chariot today?" asked an aggressive merchant from his chest mouth. He held a sharp stick in one of his many tentacles and jabbed it at them. "I'll do whatever it takes. Don't think I won't!"

Caid drew a blaster, pointing it right at the merchant. "You'll have to die."

As stunned as the merchant was by the sudden reciprocation of violence, the rest of DeepService Team One was even more taken aback.

"Christ on a cracker," Alice muttered, grabbing hold of Dan's arm for stability as she stumbled a step back.

"Come on," Caid said, "let's go." And even though they all knew that his blaster was itself a conjured hologram and no threat, they did as they were told.

The cacophony of vendors closed in around them as they continued toward the spire's tip peeking out between tents. "I can't even believe I'm asking this," Vel said, "but Caid, do you need talk about something?"

However, he seemed as placid as always now. "I always enjoy talking with you, Vel. I hope you know that. Our chats mean a lot to me."

"No, I mean, you pulled a weapon on that guy. That's something *I* would do. Maybe Alice if she's had a booster in the last hour."

"Huh?" said Alice.

Caid beamed at the lieutenant. "I knew what you meant. Part of my job is learning to speak the same language as those I encounter. I'm starting to believe there is only one language spoken in Star Cluster B, and it's not English."

Alice's brows pinched together. "It's not? Then ... how am I—?"

Dan leaned in. "He means violence. It's a figure of speech."

"Ah. Right. Of course. So this is all ... English."

"Yes, Captain."

"I thought so."

The market wasn't so much a place of commerce as an incubator for fistfights and shouting matches. Aubert got into two loud arguments that escalated quickly to death threats, but each time Vel stepped in to offer a threat of violence so great, both parties were immediately humbled and subdued. It was truly her pleasure to grab the client by the throat and drag him away from each encounter.

The lieutenant would've been tempted to let the altercations turn into violence, in the hopes that things didn't go well for Aubert, were it not for the fact that *Emergence* was still charging, and they were stuck on this planet until the ship could recuperate. In the meantime, Aubert was their only guide through the hodgepodge of merchants selling absolute crap and threatening those who declined to purchase. So, unfortunately, he needed to survive a little while longer.

"Ah, there it is!" Aubert pointed to a high stone wall ahead of them. "That's the way into the palace grounds!"

"Am I missing where the door is?" Alice asked.

"It's not far. Not far at all."

They began walking the perimeter, looking for the entrance.

The gate *was* far, but at least it was open. Inside, locals lounged on massive blankets that covered every inch of ground, and Alice was relieved to see a little bit of color variation in the natural landscape after the fifty shades of dirt that had surrounded them since their crash landing.

Unlike the rest of the arid land, the space inside the gates had flowing liquid—Alice presumed it was water, but she couldn't have been more wrong—bubbling from fountains and flowing in small streams that snaked between the blankets.

Now in friendlier territory, Alice felt emboldened to lead the way toward the palace steps, taking in the sights. Almost every one of the loungers looked human. Or Yoken. Close enough. An older gentleman leaned down and cupped some of the flowing liquid to his lips before drinking it deeply, sighing, and lying serenely on his blanket again, staring up at the sky.

How refreshing that must be, Alice thought, unaware that drinking the liquid was the preferred way of killing oneself on Trauna.

While getting inside the gates had been no hassle at all, once they reached the steps of the palace itself, half a dozen guards stepped forward, making it clear this was not a public area.

Such a thing was becoming routine for Alice, and it didn't rattle her nearly as much as it had the first time she'd encountered it on Bacc'nalia.

"We're DeepService Team One," she said. "We come on

behalf of the Depot with a request to meet with Emperor Best."

"No one has mentioned anything about that to us," said the guard closest to Alice.

"That's because we didn't tell anyone we were coming. Can you just send word up the chain to him? Let him know his envoy Aubert Orleans is with us."

The lead guard eyed them appraisingly, his gaze lingering on Vel, then roaming up and down her figure, as a sly grin blossomed.

Alice looked at her lieutenant, fully expecting there to be a blaster battle about to break out, but instead, Vel winked at the guard.

He puffed up. "Of course you're welcome. I'll inform the emperor."

"I hate this void-sucked planet," Vel muttered.

"You really need to learn the word 'fuck,' Susy."

"I know what it fucking means."

Alice backed off, and a moment later the doors opened to them, and the crew stepped inside the palace.

A wave of cold air hit Alice's skin as she crossed the threshold. "Does this place have air conditioning?"

Dan shot her a sideways glance. "Air conditioning is generally among the first technological advances on any planet this hot."

"My planet was this hot," she said, "and it took centuries before we had it."

"Yeah, well," Dan said offhandedly, taking in their new surroundings, "Blerg VFP69 has other things going for it. It's quite pretty, for instance."

The inside of the palace looked nothing like the worn-down exterior. This part of Trauna might only possess scant natural resources, but the ones it did have were condensed in this single location.

A slick white tile with ornate gold accents covered the walls, and below their feet something resembling marble stretched through the entrance hall. Alice had seen houses like this before, but only ever in the historical films about plantation life that one of her exes was a little too into.

"Please tell me that's not ghasselite," Alice whispered to Vel, glaring at the nearby banister.

"Make a claim you believe is true," Vel replied.

"You winked at that guard."

Vel growled. "Yes, that happened."

Alice chuckled victoriously. "Where did they get all these materials, anyway?"

"Maybe the planet has, you know, variation."

"Ah," said Alice, "that's possible."

Something in a miniskirt wobbled into the entrance hall from another corridor. If a slug grew four legs and then learned to walk on its back two, it would look a little like this new arrival, who seemed to be in a rush.

Besides the miniskirt, it wore nothing on top, which left Alice with quite a few questions, but she canned them for the time being.

"My name is Fint. Who are you?" The slugly thing grasped a clipboard and hovered a writing utensil above it, waiting for a reply.

"I'm Captain Alice Luck of the DeepService Team One." As Alice continued the introduction, Fint scribbled furiously on the clipboard.

"Fine, I'll see if Emperor Best has time to meet with you. He's very busy being the best, you know."

"Uh."

Fint slithered away, and the crew was left waiting.

"What, no taco service?" Alice said. "This place blows." When she saw Aubert's face turning red, she changed the subject, tapping a finger to her ear comm. "Allura."

And in the faintest whisper, "Yes ... Daddy?"

Ah, she'd forgotten. "Never mind. Rest up. We'll need you fully charged when we're undoubtedly run off this planet by an angry mob who we didn't thank profusely enough." Alice turned to her crew. "Anyone have a guess at how much time we have left in the mission?"

Dan and Vel shook their heads, and Caid said, "Forty-nine hours and twenty-six minutes ship time."

Alice blinked at him. "You sure?"

"Yes."

"How?"

"It's something I can do. Half of my strings exist on the outside of the universe, so time dilation and relativity don't mess with my perception as much. Plus, I've existed for ... Well, it's hard to describe the duration, since that varies by location."

Fint returned.

("That took three minutes and nine seconds Trauna time," Caid whispered.)

"Emperor Best has time to meet with you in two hours in the banquet hall. Until then, he requests that you enjoy the famous palace showers in the guest residences to freshen up after your long trip."

"That sounds wonderful," Aubert replied.

"Yep, that works for us," Alice added. But when she looked around at the group, it seemed Aubert was alone in his enthusiasm.

Fair enough. It was always awkward the first time you showered at someone else's house.

Fint led them down a long hallway, past alcoves with

artwork that made little sense to Alice but was undoubtedly expensive.

After recognizing the first few murals and holograms they passed as infamously stolen, Dan decided to pretend there was no artwork in this place. The less he knew, the less guilty he would feel in keeping it a secret to avoid an intergalactic incident.

It was as they passed a massive mural with the letters SC-B inscribed on a plaque beneath it that Alice remembered the bell that had rung in her mind immediately before their ship was attacked.

Star Cluster B was abbreviated SC-B.

And on the underside of the table in her laboratory were the letters SC A written in radical redshift marker.

Was that what SC A meant? Not South Carolina, but Star Cluster? Was there a Star Cluster A somewhere? The existence of a Star Cluster B certainly implied it.

And then what? What was some significance to it? Why would whoever'd used the lab before her go to the effort of writing that, presumably for someone else to find?

SC A was only the start. Do not play their game.

The start of what? Whose game?

The hallway opened up to sunshine ahead, and they stepped out onto a covered walkway a moment later. The path split off in a dozen directions, each leading to a small cottage. Would she get her own guest house, even for only a couple of hours? It'd be a nice, spacious change from her captain's chambers.

Before the group could split, though, Caid leaned close and muttered so Fint wouldn't overhear, "Don't undress more than you would in public—the odds of your being recorded in the bath for nefarious purposes are as close to one hundred percent as experimentally possible."

"Are you serious?"
He nodded somberly.
"But that's psychot— Ah."
She'd almost forgotten which star cluster they were in.

"Are you serious?"
He nodded somberly.
"But that's psychot— Ah."
She'd almost forgotten which star cluster they were in.

CHAPTER
SIXTEEN

Vel didn't need Caid's advice about remaining mostly clothed in the guest houses. She rinsed her face to clear it of the rusty dirt that had accumulated from the day, soaked her feet in a basin, and called it good.

The remaining alone time left her restless. She was beginning to doubt herself, something that had a history of leading her into a sudden nosedive. She was never one to force positivity into her brain where it didn't belong, but when the cruel and callous voice in her head, which sounded strangely like her father (she would die before letting Caid catch wind of that) found its way into her thoughts, she knew better than to allow it to keep speaking. What could she distract herself with now, though? Maybe she could return to the market and invite hand-to-hand combat with a few merchants. That would shut him up.

But no. She needed to think. There was too much to think about, and she'd been delaying it for too long.

Had she been crazy suggesting they come directly to Star Cluster B? She hadn't expected Captain Luck to agree to it so readily. But it seemed the captain was beginning to trust her, to look to her for input—you know, like a captain should their lieutenant.

And now they'd crash-landed on this deathtrap of a planet as a result.

You only ruin things, Susy. You try too hard, and then you ruin everything around you.

Fortunately, Trauna was the single planet in the entire cluster where she wanted to be. Not because it was a nice place to spend a holiday, but because it might hold clues to what happened to the original DeepService Team One, the GeneticExcellence Squad. It might answer the questions that had weighed heavy on her mind since her time in the Alliance's clutches.

Astra Blum and the other rebels hadn't held Vel for long, but it was long enough for them to plant the seed. Astra, the leader of that faction, had spoken with her directly. Not interrogated her, precisely, but questioned her. And the questions were odd.

Once Vel had the time to reflect and process on their vacation to Jaspariampt, the questions had morphed from odd to sinister, and her mind demanded she make sense of them.

The Alliance had treated her well, fed her, kept her hydrated. What had felt hostile at the time—for instance, springing upon her and kidnapping her from Location— seemed necessary and understandable upon later examination. It was something she could see herself doing out of necessity. She'd certainly done much worse in the wars.

Then again, the Alliance had tried to assassinate the crew on Bacc'nalia. But when Vel spat that ugly fact at her captors, Astra had denied it adamantly, seemed genuinely confused when the accusation was hurled her way.

The main answer Astra was after was what the Depot wanted from DeepService Team One. What was the mission? Why? Who was the crew's handler? How did they select the clients they took on?

The questions seemed so asinine, so unimportant, that Vel had considered providing honest answers. But she knew what a captor was worth. If she gave up the information, however useless it might prove, she'd lost her use except to lure her crew into a trap.

And so Vel had refused to divulge a thing, expecting the response to be violence.

But it wasn't. The only pain she'd endured was when two men who looked like giant rats snuck into her cell after the questioning and tried to have a little fun with her. She fought them off with the legs of the chair she was tied to, taking a few licks in the process. When Astra came charging into the room to discover what her men were doing, she'd blasted a hole through one man's foot to send a clear message. Then, to Vel's shock, Astra apologized for her guards' behavior.

What kind of a kidnapper did that? It was inconceivable. She'd never experienced that sort of compassion from an enemy. It made no sense.

After hours of questioning, to which Vel remained an impenetrable force field, Astra Blum left her with a final thought: *Go to Star Cluster B. Seek out Trauna. Find the original DeepService Team One there. If you want to find us afterward and talk, put out a blast with the word "chorus" and we'll find you.*

Vel entered the banquet hall ten minutes ahead of the established meeting time with Emperor Best. Caid was already there, likely because bathing of any kind was out of the question for him.

The hall resembled an upscale restaurant dining room,

with round tables scattered about, accommodating up to eight people each, many of them already occupied by elegantly dressed parties. Who the void these people were, though, Vel didn't know or care.

She took a seat next to Caid.

"How was the bath?" he asked.

"I kept it to my face and feet."

"This seems like a place where footage of feet would be enough."

Vel waved it off. "Let them try to enjoy it. These feet spent three years slogging through swampy muck in tactical boots that didn't fit. If someone can get off on looking at them, good for that person."

"Far be it from me to assume what knowledge and lessons your life journey has taught you, but from my experience in the multiverse, feet are a rare commodity. The vast majority of life forms are footless, let alone *toeless*. Many are not picky about the state of the feet. Some even pay more for the rougher ones."

"Depths of the universe, Caid! I wish someone had told me that *before* I signed with the Depot. I could've retired early."

Caid laughed, gazing at a silent collection of adults a table over. The rubbery slug one was so tense and rigid, it wasn't jiggling, not even a quiver. "All the riches in this palace, but not enough to buy happiness." He turned his attention to Vel. "How are you feeling?"

She shot a sideways look at the hologram. "Are we starting a therapy session?"

He smiled gently. "No. I'm asking my friend how she's doing."

She relaxed. "I'm fine, as usual."

"Really? Because if I remember correctly, it was at your

mysterious suggestion and prodding that we came to Star Cluster B, and by many metrics, it's not exactly going well. If I know you at all, you're blaming yourself for it."

She shrugged a single shoulder. "So what if I am?"

That gave the guy pause, much to Vel's satisfaction. Finally, he said, "Don't?"

She chuckled. "If you say so. Hey, while I have you to myself …"

"You can always see me in my—"

She waved off his response. "How many DeepService Teams have you worked with?"

Caid pressed his hands to his heart. "Many."

"Were you always the therapist?"

"No. Not at all. Mental health support is something I sort of fell into after a while. I was providing it anyway, and they decided to create a position that I then filled."

Vel drummed her fingers on her thigh, thinking hard. Caid knew things about the Depot's purpose that even Liz Windsor might not, but only through roundabout ways that didn't hit the tripwire of patient confidentiality could she access information that might prove helpful to putting together this unsettling puzzle. "Before they assigned you to mental health, what did you do?"

"I was in charge of diplomacy. What Dan is now. They recruited specifically for a hologram to fill the position. I'd recently finished a residency at the Glou'tth Nebula Universal Peace Institute Commune, and I was looking for the next step. One of my friends told me about the opening, and it … *resonated* with me." He winked playfully.

"Why do you think they were looking specifically for a hologram?"

"I stood no danger of being killed. Diplomacy can sometimes go south, so they wanted someone who couldn't be blasted to dark matter. It's like what Alice has me do. And for the record, I don't mind being the decoy if it helps my friends. But it quickly became clear I wasn't right for the position. Much of diplomacy includes accepting food and drinks, and since I can't, my inability was often taken as an insult, even after I explained my circumstance to some of the beings who hadn't before encountered an organic hologram." He chuckled. "Man, we found ourselves in some sticky spots because of it. I would go in, build rapport with the hosts, and they would assume I was in charge of the mission—if not in an official sense, in a ceremonial one. Then when I couldn't eat the food, couldn't even lift the utensils? Ha!" He shook his head fondly. "Yeah, I was shot so many times. *So* many. Lost count."

Though Vel was glad he didn't take any of it personally, she wasn't there to relive a highlight reel. She was there for the lowlights. That was where the useful information hid. "Caid, have you ever been to Star Cluster B before?"

His words felt measured as she sensed the wall come up. "No, I have not."

"You've given me no reason to believe you'd lie. But I also feel like there's more you're not telling me."

"If there was more I could—"

She held up a hand to stop him, attention shifting to where Captain Luck was striding in, her blonde hair still slightly damp.

The captain plunked down in a seat across the table from them. "I feel like a new woman!"

"You ... bathed?" Caid asked.

"Sure did. Don't regret it at all. Oh, I mean, I heard what you said about not taking off clothes, but the cat's already out of the bag for me. Not on purpose, mind you. We had community showers in my dorm freshman year, and those things used to get clogged with hair constantly." She paused, her eyes glazing over momentarily. "Or maybe that was just what we were told." She shook off the concern. "Either way, the plumber was in and out of there all the time. We found out during my senior year that he wasn't a plumber at all. He was filming us and selling it. He had to keep going in there to switch out the tapes. No one caught him for years, and most of those tapes were already long gone by the time he was burned. I'd bet if you did a search for 'stocky blonde barely legal shower College Station,' my videos would pop up." She gripped her ponytail at the base and dragged her hand down, squeezing the excess water onto the floor beside her chair. "Anyway, these baths were too tempting. You wouldn't believe all the red dirt that came off me. Looked like a horror film in there."

Dan arrived right at the scheduled time to meet the emperor.

As he sat, he turned a concerned expression to Alice. "You showered?"

"We've already been over it," Vel informed him. "She did it with full consent."

As minutes ticked by and still no sign of the emperor or Aubert Orleans, a restlessness settled on the table.

"I'm sure he's a busy man," Dan muttered, rocking slightly in his seat.

When Aubert arrived, nearly a quarter of an hour late, Dan's anxiety had turned to impatience. "You're late."

Aubert turned up his nose. "I'm not late so long as I'm here before Emperor Best."

"Yeah, well," Alice muttered, "he may be Emperor Best, but he's the *worst* at being on time." Her stomach growled. "Maybe we should go ahead and order."

Dan nixed that immediately as the wrong way to start

diplomatic relations. Vel shot a look at Caid, who subtly nodded his support of the decision.

It was another quarter of an hour when Fint entered the banquet room, no clipboard this time. "Emperor Best apologizes for the delay," she announced. "He will be with you shortly."

"How short?" Alice asked.

"Five minutes at the most."

The captain had slumped down in her chair, her butt on the very edge, at serious risk of sliding off in her battle to suppress the urge to leave. But now she scooted back, sat up straight. "Oh, that's not bad."

Fint wobbled away again.

"What's the plan, Captain?" asked Dan.

"How many times do I have to tell you that I don't have one?" Alice grabbed one of the expensive metal forks and wiggled it between her thumb and pointer, trying to make it look like rubber. "I do have a *goal*," she added. "And that's to find out more about what's going on with the population, why it's not growing."

"What," Aubert said bitterly, "I couldn't provide you with enough information?"

She tossed the fork onto the table. "No, you couldn't. I thought that might be made obvious by the fact that we're here to get more information."

Fint re-entered the banquet hall half an hour later. "Only another five minutes," she said. "He's terribly sorry about the delay. But he was about to head this way when I left him."

Alice said nothing this time, just stared at Fint through bored, glassy eyes.

Dan spoke up. "Then I suppose we should continue to wait until he arrives to begin our meal."

"Yes," Fint confirmed, "that is the custom here."

Once she'd left again, Aubert said, "This is a gross insult."

"For once," Alice said, "I agree with you. He's left us waiting for over an hour. Maybe we should dine and dash."

"No," Vel said quickly. "If we leave without speaking to him, what was the point of coming all this way?"

No one had a good answer, and so the crew settled in once again.

But an hour later, when Fint returned for the third time, even Vel had had enough.

"Ten more minutes."

"You told us he was about to walk down here the last time," Alice said. "Whatever happened to that?"

"He's assured me it will only be ten more minutes. He's just finished up an important communication with the council of a nearby planet, and he's on his way out the door of his chambers at this very moment."

But as Fint turned to leave, Alice rose from her seat. "Nah, we're done waiting." When Vel shot her a concerned look, she added, "I'll figure something out, don't worry."

Her track record of thinking on her feet had become compelling, or at least compelling enough in the present conditions, and the rest of the group was happy to follow the captain's lead, rising from their seats.

Alice was almost out of the banquet hall when a large man in bright orange and gold robes stepped inside. He looked entirely human, and were Alice not already so annoyed with him, she might've found him attractive the way she'd first found Aubert appealing. He had soft brown eyes, midnight skin, and high cheekbones that could surely cut glass.

He also had an air about him that made it clear who he was.

And the crew had a look about them that made it clear who they were. Namely, the jumpsuits.

The emperor scanned Alice up and down, then Vel, his eyes pausing briefly on the Depot insignia.

Aubert stepped forward, shoving his way between the captain and lieutenant. "Emperor Best! It is my honor to see you again. I thought you'd be dead by the time I returned, but it appears you've only aged a decade!"

The emperor looked down his perfectly symmetrical nose at the man. "Who in reality are you?"

A horror-stricken expression pounced upon Aubert's face before the magenta of indignation could replace it a moment later. "I'm the *envoy* appointed to work with the Depot's DeepService Team One."

"And this is that team?" Emperor Best said, his voice sagging with boredom.

"Yes, Emperor."

"It looks like they were leaving without meeting with me. How very *rude*." He directed his distaste at Vel, making the same mistake that the Alliance had about who was in charge. Too annoyed to respond, Vel deferred to the real captain.

"We waited for you for over two hours," Alice said. "Where I come from, wasting people's time is an insult. We have limited time per mission, you know. We came here to better serve your people, and you're treating us like that pile of laundry that needs to be folded—leaving us slouched on chairs far longer than you said you would. Now, I thank you for setting us up in the guest houses for a nice scrub, but we're in a time squeeze, and we need to get to fixing our ship and completing this mission ... for *you*."

Emperor Best looked her up and down again. "You bathed?"

She glared back at him.

"Did you … bathe your feet as well?" He licked his lips as his gaze dropped to her Texas flag boots like he might crack them open and eat what was inside.

"The hell?" Alice muttered. But she already understood. There was a film director out of Austin who felt similarly about feet, as one of her girlfriends had discovered the unfortunate way at a party a few years back.

Vel also didn't miss the way the emperor gawked at Alice's boots, and despite her previous sentiments, she suddenly wished she *had* stuck to washing her face.

"Excuse us," Alice said, "we've got somewhere to be." She stepped to the side to pass him.

"Wait!" The emperor's soft brown eyes grew hard, and Alice thought she saw a sliver of yellow appear down the middle, like a fissure in the earth. "I have time to meet now. But not here. Come with me to my suite and I'll answer all your questions. I'll have Fint bring you some food."

Alice put her back to the emperor, deferring to her team. Vel was the first to give silent consent with a small slackening of her shoulders. Caid pressed his palms together and bowed slightly, and shortly after, Dan shrugged. Aubert might've given a signal, but Alice didn't care to check.

"Fine," she said, "but the food better be good."

She could really go for another plate of quadruple-decker tacos.

CHAPTER
SEVENTEEN

It probably goes without saying that there is no multiversal standard of beauty, no perfect ratio of eyes to mouth or antennae to suckers. True symmetry is rare, and there are many combinations of features that become *more* threatening when presented with something close to symmetry.

A being named Thannoo once dedicated his life to creating a formula that could predict sexual attractiveness in any creature, any species, any configuration of parts.

They came very close with $1/(A \times T)$, where A equals the number of standard deviations away from the average features of the being's kind and T equals the being's percent chance of successfully killing another of its species. The higher the result, the greater the attractiveness. One's ability to kill another of its species was too difficult to calculate, however. If Thennoo calculated based on strength and agility, it became easier, but they couldn't mathematically account for sneakiness.

No one ever can.

They took a different approach next, incorporating

variables for the placement of vision sensors on the body, visible signs of poor health, and distance traveled by natural smell. All of this took Thannoo much closer to the true formula, but still they failed.

When they lay on their deathbed, centuries later, they experienced an epiphany.

Thannoo's last words were "A scale of one to ten."

It was so nearly a perfect system for measuring beauty that it traveled through the multiverse at quantum speeds.

However, it still had one fatal flaw, one variable Thannoo had failed to take into account, that was perhaps the most important: C.

Which represents *communication*.

The more Emperor Best opened his mouth, the less attractive Alice found him.

On their walk to the private room to discuss the details of their mission, he did nothing but brag about the art they passed and whom he had to know to attain it.

Alice didn't know any of the people he mentioned, but she recognized obnoxious name dropping when she heard it.

The walls of the private room they entered were absolutely covered with portraits of the emperor. While the artistic styles and techniques varied, the subject did not. In the first that Alice inspected, he was riding one of the weird pear animals; in another he was shaking hands with a being half his size and mostly made up of ... blades?

Didn't matter. The point was that Alice found herself in the presence of too many Emperor Bests for her liking. One was too many.

While not a particularly punctual person herself, Alice mostly *tried* to be on time. Punctuality was a hard practice to master; she understood that. Sometimes fun opportunities presented themselves out of nowhere, and what was she going to do, skip them for something lame like seeing a doctor or her college graduation? Please.

But, fun opportunities aside, she did try to be on time. And the emperor's extreme tardiness had gotten under her skin. Burrowed there and dug its claws in. She was the captain of DeepService Team One. She represented the Depot, which seemed to be a big deal in the vast reaches of space. She deserved a little goddamn respect.

It was a good thing she didn't hold her breath for it.

The portrait room, as she'd come to think of it despite every room likely having this many depictions of Best, was also a sitting room. But even that didn't quite match the functionality, because it was only a sitting room for Emperor Best, who settled in comfortably on a large, padded, jewel-embellished chair. For the rest of them, it was a crouching room.

With a regal sweep of his arm, he motioned for them to make themselves comfortable on low three-legged stools arranged in a semicircle around him. When Alice did (reluctantly), she could've rested her chin on her knees. Vel, who had a few inches on the captain, and most of that pegs, looked like she was midair, shouting "cannonball!" It was clear from the lieutenant's expression, however, that if she shouted such a thing in this moment, it would've been because she was firing one at the emperor's gut.

"I've sired fifteen hundred children," the emperor said, picking at a plate of colorful and ripe fruit on the armrest of his chair—a plate he'd clearly been picking at prior to meeting them in the banquet hall.

"Fifteen hundred?" Dan asked, feigning interest. His back was curled in a perfect C, the ridges of his armor straining against the fabric of his Depot shirt.

"Yes," said the emperor, "fifteen hundred, give or take."

"So *you* don't have any sort of fertility troubles?" Alice said, keenly aware that she was only beginning to comprehend how dangerous it was to discuss infertility with powerful and powerfully insecure figures. But it was her job, and really, these people needed to get over it.

"I have no fertility troubles at all. Almost *too* fertile." Best laughed, taking the opportunity to pop another snack bite into his open mouth. "Can't enjoy a single wallop without the thing getting pregnant!"

"You are the very best at walloping," Aubert said, laughing along. He looked down the row at the crew. "This guy is a legend. Seriously."

As much as Alice hadn't loved Aubert's bitter and competitive side, she liked his sycophantic side even less.

"That's great," she said, grimace-smiling. "Super awesome. Yeah."

"I bet I've even walloped your wife!" exclaimed the emperor, pointing viciously at Aubert.

"I don't have a wife," Aubert said. "Otherwise, yeah, you probably would've."

"No wife?! What a piss-poor existence! I have twenty! Not a single one has left me! A few have tried, but I walloped them all into submission!" The emperor guffawed. "One of them even died with the walloping I gave her! That'll show her! I replaced her with my advisor's wife. Walloped her in front of him, too!"

Aubert's eyes were wide with eager envy and admiration, which Alice knew in her heart of hearts was a signal to slow this down a bit, to put on the brakes and get caught up on what she might be missing. A quick look at the thinly veiled horror on Dan's face only confirmed it.

"I'm not familiar with that term, wallop," she said. "Well, I am, but I think I means something different where I come from."

"Earth!" Emperor Best declared. "A planet that deigns to call itself one of the elements! You come from everybody's favorite Blerg VFP69, correct? Origination of the Depot itself!"

"Yessir."

"Yessir, she says to me! Perfect! I have half a mind to wallop you right here, in front of all your crew. They wouldn't mind, would they?"

Perhaps he was expecting a different reaction from the stone-still horror of Vel, Dan, and Caid, but he cleared his throat quickly and returned to the topic at hand. "What does wallop mean on Earth?"

Alice's mind traveled back to some of the wallopings she'd received for sneaking around with boys or coming home too late or using the Lord's name in vain. "It means someone whoops you. Really knocks the snot out of you. Leaves bruises. That kinda thing."

"I see the meaning hasn't been warped during interplanetary travel," said Emperor Best. "It means the same here."

"So you impregnate other Yoken by … beating them up?" They looked so incredibly human, though. Could she have somehow assumed the genitals functioned the same when they didn't? How in the hell could impregnation be completed through hand-to-hand combat?

Emperor Best guffawed. "Not just beating them up, no! There's more to it. I also I insert myself into the woman while I beat her. That completes the walloping ceremony."

Alice couldn't have gotten her mouth to shut if she'd given it her full attention. That was the most generous use of the word "ceremony" she'd ever heard. But maybe, yet again, she'd missed something, placed an assumption somewhere it ought not be …

She turned to Dan, hoping he could shed some light on the glaring miscommunication between cultures. But he only exhaled deeply and let his eyes fall closed. She turned to the next likely candidate for making sense of Emperor Best's explanation, because *surely* she'd gotten something about it wrong.

But Aubert Orleans seemed to have heard nothing out of the ordinary and flashed her a cheesy grin when she looked directly at him.

Vel stared at the emperor with the placidness of a pond's surface … while a hungry gator lurked below. It was the single immaterial tear sliding down Caid's cheek that solidified it for Alice.

She wasn't missing anything. "So you … When you engage in sex, you also *beat the snot out of the woman?*"

"You say it like I have a choice."

"I fail to see how you don't."

"Then let me enlighten you," replied the emperor, speaking slowly as if the speed of communication was the major problem. "If I didn't wallop her"—he mimed a fighting motion with his fist—"she'd get away." With two fingers, he mimicked bipedal legs running.

"Sweet Jesus," said Alice.

Emperor Best raised an interested eyebrow. "Now *you* have used a word I don't understand. What is Jesus? It sounds scrumptious."

"It's a who," Alice replied, her temples throbbing, "and it's no one you'd enjoy, so don't worry about it."

Mercifully, Dan stepped in. "Emperor Best, would you say that your habits in regard to, um, *walloping* are typical of male Yoken?"

"And some of the females and intersex, yes! But they usually do it for fun, to pretend, roleplay. The males do it because it comes *naturally* to us. We were made this way."

Alice glared at the man who appeared to be as Homo sapiens as she was. "You've inflicted sex on women at least fifteen hundred times, then. Is that *also* typical?"

"No, no. Of course not. Mine is a great achievement—however, I also have more access than the average Yoken to females as well as males and the intersex. And they like me better because, well, look at me!"

"You make it sound like they're happy to be walloped by you, but if that were the case, maybe you wouldn't have to *wallop* them?"

"It's a poorly kept secret," replied Best, "that the women *love* being walloped. Secretly crave it."

"It's true!" Aubert confirmed. "Everybody knows it's their secret desire."

Alice swallowed around the growing pit in her stomach and reminded herself she'd worked worse jobs for far less pay. Only after revisiting a memory of waiting tables at that sports bar during UFC Fight Night and being tipped five percent on each tab was she able to press on. "So, the average male on your planet sires ... how many children, do you think?"

Get the information then get the hell out of here.

"We haven't collected data on that, but anecdotally, two to three hundred."

That didn't sound like a population problem to her, or rather it was of the opposite nature that concerned DeepService Team One. She turned to Aubert. "That sound about right to you?" Because it couldn't be, right? The exponential curve would look like a straight vertical line within a generation.

"Definitely," Aubert confirmed. "I'm a young guy, and I've sired about a hundred and fifty—mind you, I've been *extremely* busy with my work lately. Hardly any time for walloping."

Vel stepped in. "Apologies for my confusion, Emperor Best, but we walked through a crowded marketplace not five hours ago, and I saw only a few adolescent beings. But if the Yoken are as fertile as you say—and I have no reason to believe you're lying about it—then I have to ask: where are all these children?"

The emperor didn't hesitate. "Dead, mostly."

"Oh."

Dismissing it with a bored flick of his wrist, Emperor Best continued. "They're fragile things, that's the problem. They need so much *coddling*. Can't do anything on their own, as I understand it. When I was young, nobody helped me. I was the void-swallowed emperor's son, and they still left me to figure it out on my own. But look at me now! I turned out great. Better for it, in fact!"

Maybe they are *a perfect match with the splatterpoots,* Alice thought. Neither one cared much if their offspring lived or died, only that the population growth remained steady. How they expected one thing without the other was beyond her enormous pay grade to understand, though.

"Out of curiosity, Emperor Best," she said, "how many offspring did your father produce?"

"Emperor Better?" He chuckled. "The man was a legend. He set the record of fifty-six hundred. Multiple women a night over the span of his long life."

"And how many of his offspring are still alive?"

"Last I checked? Eight. Including me."

Reproduction was officially a numbers game on Trauna, one they were all incredibly unskilled at playing. "And how many children can a single woman gestate at once?"

"Two."

"Tell me if I've got this straight. Your people experience no issue in fertility. The problem is that once the baby has been born, its odds of survival are ... almost zero?"

The emperor squeezed one of his juicy snacks in his fist until it exploded. "How dare you speak in that tone of judgment, Captain Luck."

Alice tried not to sigh too obviously. She was growing tired of fragile leaders. "I'm trying to get all the facts, Emperor Best. Not judging at all."

She was. She definitely was.

"For your information, we believe in equal rights on Trauna! To expect a woman to give up everything to raise a child she never asked for would be *cruel*."

She didn't buy it. She'd dated too many male feminists in her lifetime to fall for rookie-level lip service. "But the walloping? The impregnation against her will? That's just *natural*, huh?"

Emperor Best puffed up his chest. "Yes. It's what males of our species do."

"And the women who have been walloped, do they have any choice but to take the child to full term?"

"I don't understand what you mean."

Yikes. This was a topic she didn't especially like getting into back on Earth, where she mostly understood the cultural norms. But here ...

Fuck it. She forged on. "Do the women have the option of terminating the pregnancies they never asked for?"

"Terminating?! What a crass way of describing murder. And no, we don't tolerate that treatment of our unborn."

Caid reached over and set a steadying hand on her thigh, and though it mostly moved through her, she appreciated the gesture.

"I believe I follow," Alice said, "but I want to make sure I have a clear picture of the situation before we move forward: the males of your species wallop unwilling females regularly, and then the females are forced to give birth, at which point they want nothing to do with the child and, what, just leave it someplace to figure life out for itself?"

"If the woman survives the pregnancy, yes."

Alice blinked. "Why do you say it like that?"

"Pregnant women are slow."

She looked to Dan for a clue, but he appeared as lost as she was. "They're … slow?"

"Yes! Slow! Slow! They lack speed and agility and can be easily caught and murdered by drifters."

"By drifters?!" Alice jumped to her feet. "The hell is happening in these parts?"

"We have a huge drifter problem." The emperor shrugged. "What can you do?"

"Drifters gonna drift," Aubert added unhelpfully.

"If they're murdering women—" Alice began, but Best cut her off.

"Not all women!" He slapped his armrest. "Only the pregnant ones! Don't you think if we had drifters murdering *all* women, we would do something about it?"

Alice's mouth fell open. She met Vel's eyes, and that was all she needed. Her horror was reflected back to her in the dilated pupils of a war veteran.

She addressed the emperor on his throne. "This whole goddamn planet is fucking soulless. Jesus! You force women to have targets on their backs and get hunted by drifters, then you try to act righteous about … *anything?* Why would anyone in their right mind want to match you with another species? Pure genocide. It would be pure goddamn genocide!"

Dan scrambled to his feet, stepping between his captain and the emperor. "What she means to say—"

Alice shoved him aside with her injured arm and cringed. The pain only emboldened her. "What I mean to say is that this planet and everyone on it can get fucked. You don't have a birth problem, you have a living problem, and we can't help you with that." She turned to the others. "We're outta here."

"Captain Luck," Dan protested, but Vel shoved him firmly after their leader, who was halfway out the door already.

The meeting was over.

And so was this mission.

CHAPTER
EIGHTEEN

"You walked out on Emperor Best," Aubert Orleans said frantically as they stomped through the blanketed palace lawn.

Alice ignored him and kept walking. This place was making her feel claustrophobic, and she suspected it had less to do with the high walls surrounding it and more to do with, ya know, all the rapists, of which Aubert Orleans was one.

Once they were back in the bustle of the dusty marketplace, free of the lounging citizens and toxic flowing streams, Alice felt a hand grip her shoulder, and she turned and found herself eye to eye with their loathsome client.

It took every last ounce of control for her to keep her elbow from meeting his quivering chin.

One time, in a country on Blerg VFP69 known as the United States, which was a deeply ironic name once you got to know a little bit about it, there was a high court called the Supreme Court. There was also an item at a popular food dispensary called a Crunchwrap Supreme. The two things were similar in more ways than many inhabitants of the United States would ever understand.

Among the processes of the Supreme Court was ushering in new members after the old ones spent a few decades slipping into dementia on the job and eventually died. During one of these proceedings, which Alice missed because she was in outer space at the time, a man much like Aubert Orleans in heart and disposition was eligible to take the position on this highest court. And when the people of the United States asked him about trying to wallop an incapacitated woman in his earlier years, he made a face similar to the one Aubert Orleans made at Alice then—corners of the mouth turned down in an unpleasant scowl, chin quivering with indignation, eyes like two change-purse zippers, cheeks flushed with the passionate memory of walloping.

Her elbow jerked once at her side like a chicken wing, but with a great effort, she wrangled it back against her body.

"You will march right back in there and apologize to the emperor," Aubert demanded, tightening his grip on Alice's shoulder.

She karate-chopped his wrist, something she had no skill in but felt was the right course of action. And it worked. Aubert jerked his hand back.

"No." She turned away from him.

"How *dare* you! You have *no* right! You'll *never* succeed in this mission now!"

She whirled on him again. "I'm not matching *anyone* with the people of Trauna."

"Wait," Dan said, positioning himself near her but not within arm's reach. "Then how are we going to complete this assignment?"

"We're *not*. How the hell could we? I've done some shady shit in my life, some real gray-area stuff, but this?"

"This is fucked," Vel said, appearing at Alice's shoulder.

Alice almost smiled despite the situation. She pointed at her second-in-command. "What she said! We were doomed from the start, don't y'all see?"

Dan wasn't ready to let it go. "But why would the Depot—"

Alice threw her hands into the air. "Anybody's guess, Dan. Who really knows why they do anything. Caid?"

The therapist, who had been observing from a few paces away, moved closer.

"What's your read on this?"

He frowned. "People don't grow unless they want to grow."

She shot him a finger gun. "Boom. What he said. I'm aborting this mission."

Dan's mouth fell open, and behind him, Aubert gasped. "You can't do that!"

"Hell yeah, I can! I'm doing it right now, you prick!"

"You'll make me look bad to the rest of the council! You bitch!" Aubert lunged at her, but Vel dropped him to the ground, his chest beneath her boot in an instant.

Alice shot her lieutenant an appreciative thumbs-up.

"We could kill him," Vel suggested. "Doubt anyone around here would care."

Alice weighed her options. "Nah. Not worth your energy."

Reluctantly, Vel removed her boot from his chest, and Aubert was up in a flash, whimpering as he streaked into the crowd and disappeared from sight.

"Captain," Dan said, trying to keep his voice steady but

doing a poor job of it. "Nothing *can't* be undone here. We can still go back to the emperor and—"

"Not happening, Dan."

"We'll be banished to the outer reaches of the universe!"

Alice wrinkled her nose, her hands on her hips as she looked around for inspiration on what to do next. "You don't *know* that."

"Liz Windsor—"

"She said that about the trial mission. She never said it about this one."

"They'll fire us at the very least!"

"You also don't know that." She set a hand on his shoulder and forced him to meet her eyes. "I've pulled *much* stupider things at my jobs before."

He blinked at her. "Without getting fired?"

"Um. Nah, I was always fired."

"We'll lose our pay," Dan continued. "What if they send you back to Earth forever?"

Alice's mind hadn't gotten that far.

The only thought that she'd had room for in her mind was that there was no way she would match any planet, even another one in Star Cluster B that was equally as messed up, with these people. She wouldn't be responsible for inflicting that much misery on any population. It wasn't an option. Nope.

But now that she began exploring the possible consequences, Dan had a point. Walking out on Emperor Best might've doomed her to the prison known as Earth for the rest of her life, where women her age were expected to be secretaries at oil companies, look like sexy teenagers forever, and have fiancés.

"I support your decision," said Caid. "Ethically, you

couldn't have made any other one. It was an act of great nonviolence."

Alice felt herself deflating. Would she be pressured to have kids back on Earth? "Thanks." She shot a glance at Vel. "Where do you fall on all this, Susy?"

"Right in step with you, Captain. This assignment was doomed from the start."

That would have to be enough, then. If Dan held any dreams of insubordination, the lieutenant's support of her decision would quash them. It was scary enough being on Vel's team. Standing against her? No thanks.

Alice cupped a palm around her ear to block out the noise of the market. "Allura, how you doing?"

"Starting to feel more myself, Daddy. But I'm afraid my left tubal clamp sustained damage in one of the hits. I'll need a new one before I can leave orbit."

"Oh damn." Alice grimaced. The hell was a tubal clamp? "Can you, um, tell Susy what it is we need?"

A finger pressed into her ear, Vel stared vaguely ahead for a moment then said, "Got it. Keep recharging, and we'll return to you in a bit."

"You know what the part is?"

"Yeah, not a big deal. Thankfully, it's something almost every ship has, and it's a fairly standard part across the models. We should be able to find something that'll work around here."

Alice's hand fell to the blaster on her belt. "Great. Let's make a deal. Then let's get the hell out of Star Cluster B."

CHAPTER
NINETEEN

"That one," said Caid as he pointed at a tall, gregarious merchant. "He'll be easy enough."

They'd found the shipyard section of the bazaar, and then it had merely been a matter of identifying the right seller to approach. They crew had lingered from a distance for a quarter of an hour, allowing Caid to do his reconnaissance. Finally, he'd chosen.

"What's our strategy?" Alice asked.

"Go up, flatter him, and inform him that you could have chosen any of his competitors, but he struck you as more of an expert in this matter. Then tell him what you're looking for, what dire circumstances you're in, and how much he would be helping you out with the sale. And only after all that do you ask him the price. He's going to quote you twice what it's worth and say he's cutting you a deal. Haggle at your own peril."

Alice waved that idea off. "I have money, remember? What I don't have is all day."

"Then accept whatever he offers, but not too quickly.

Make sure it looks like a stretch for you, or else he'll find some way to raise it. Oh, and how is your arm?"

Alice raised it and lowered it with only moderate discomfort. "Getting better quickly. Allura gave me something for it."

Caid frowned. "Topical ointment? Red bottle with orange lettering?"

Alice arched a brow at him. "Yes."

"Ah. Wish I'd known that sooner. You shouldn't be carrying a weapon right now."

"Huh?"

"You're *incredibly* high."

"I feel fine."

Dan gasped. "Was that what all that"—he waved at the palace in the distance—"was about? If so, I can simply tell Emperor Best you weren't in your right mind—"

"We've been over this. No. That was all me."

"Frankly," Vel added, "that was probably a more mellow version of you. I would've liked to see you tell him off when you *weren't* high."

"I'm not high!" Alice demanded, wishing she didn't mean it. "I only put a little on. Christ."

She'd put a lot on.

She was high.

Fortunately, the adrenaline rush of the crash landing had helped to sober her up in more ways than one.

"Fine," Caid said. "The reason I ask about the arm is that you *cannot* let whatever merchant you choose see that you're injured."

"And once we have the part?" Vel asked.

"Get out of there as quickly as possible. Run if you have to. No-contact is the best way to deal with people like this."

Alice groaned. "The word 'best' has been ruined for me.

Okay"—she clapped Dan on the back—"feel free to shoot whoever you want while we're gone."

Dan, sulking and anxious about the aborted mission, hung back with Caid and let the captain and lieutenant broker the deal. Not five minutes later, he witnessed the hand-off of the part, then Alice turned and sprinted back. Vel, never a fan of running away herself, hesitated but ultimately hurried after her captain in a show of loyalty and support.

"Okay," Alice said, slightly out of breath. "Worked like a charm. Let's get back to the ship." She took a step then paused, turned forty-five degrees, took another step, then paused again. "I might have, um ..."

"Don't worry," Vel said, clutching the tubal clamp, "I can navigate. Follow me."

Something in her tone set Dan on edge, but then again, anything would've set him on edge. More on edge, that was. Ever since Alice told off the emperor, Dan's nerves had tingled like a bad case of the quantum jitters coming on. Perhaps it was a low-grade probability wave he'd experienced, but more likely, he was scared shitless.

They were about to board their ship after *abandoning the mission*. He still couldn't believe it. The dread made it hard to breathe.

He knew the Depot probably wouldn't kill them. After all, the guys in charge *had* to know that finding a match for anyone in Star Cluster B was a long shot. In all his time working for and with the Depot in various roles, he knew the organization could be callous, but it was never *unreasonable*.

But if it is ...

No, the Depot wouldn't kill or even banish them—Alice was probably right about that. But it would certainly fire them, wouldn't it? And then what? Return home to Pangoliarch to live in the nicest cavern? Wile away his days in death sports? Create a burrow and family of his own? He shuddered at the thought. He dreamed of a comfortable life, but that was where he liked to keep it: in his dreams. To be planet-bound on a place as devoid of interesting culture as Pangoliarch was a fate worse than death.

The Ministry of Weapons and Culture wouldn't take him back after a disgrace like this, not when they were working so hard to maintain amicable relations with the Depot. What would happen next? What were his options? What terrible danger was coming for him that he hadn't yet identified?

You face one challenging client and you can't cut it. You're a fraud, Danger Zone. Why would you think you could be in charge of diplomacy when you have zero courage? You can't even stand up to your captain when she's putting your job on the line, just like you couldn't stand up to the bullies at school or your father ...

Dan's silent self-flagellation continued unabated as he slumped along behind the rest of the crew, keeping enough of an eye on Caid's feet to make sure he didn't get left behind. *If I were left behind, I would deserve it.*

Then the feet, tentacles, and globules in his line of vision disappeared fully, and he looked up. Wait. This wasn't where they'd come in.

He hustled past Alice and Caid and pulled up next to Vel. "This isn't the way to the ship."

"I know." Vel kept marching.

"You're supposed to be taking us back to the ship." Why was everyone acting unreasonably today?

"I will. But there's no hurry now that we've decided to abort the mission."

"I'm in a hurry to get off this void-swallowed planet, aren't you?"

"Would you relax?"

"We're going to be fired, Vel! That doesn't"—he tripped over a scampering shrub, which yelped—"that doesn't bother you at all?"

"If I'm right about my hunch, being fired is the least of our worries."

"Huh?! How is that supposed to make me feel better about anything? And what hunch? Where are you taking us?"

"I have to see if they were telling the truth."

"If *who* was telling the truth? Because I can assure you that if the 'they' refers to anyone on this planet, the answer is no, they were *not* telling the truth. There! Question answered!"

She stopped walking and turned to him. "I appreciate your caution. It's a delight to have around when our captain is … you know."

"I do. And I *also* know that you're going along with her right now. What I don't know is why."

"Maybe you'll understand in a minute." Vel's fingers brushed the blaster at her hip. "There's a lot going on we haven't been told."

As she began her march again, Dan muttered, "Maybe it's better that way."

***

Vel paused as a large, rusty hill rose up in front of them. Alice broke off her conversation with Caid to look around. "Uh, Susy? This doesn't look familiar *at all*."

Yes, the hill still had the same ruddy hue that Alice had

come to expect, but there were a few notable features that didn't ring a bell—dark green shrubs that *didn't* scurry around and large toadstools with dangerous orange markings. She thought she would've noticed those things if she'd seen them before, even if ghasselite was around.

Vel tore off a stick from one of the scrubs, which moaned in ecstasy as she did, and dragged the tip of it through the dirt. Alice realized she was writing, and her mind jumped back to the radical redshift marker under the laboratory table.

She stood next to the lieutenant to see what she'd written in the dirt:

COMMS OFF

Alice waved over the other two, pressed a finger to her lips, and pointed.

One by one, each member of DeepService Team One followed orders, shut off their earpieces, and cut themselves off from the rest of the multiverse.

(Except, of course, Caid, who was one with everything all the time but not in a snitch sort of way.)

Dan was the first to speak, mostly to himself: "This isn't a good sign."

"All right, Susy, you got something. Spill," Alice said.

"There are trackers in our comms. They'll update with the history once we reconnect. We need to leave them here before we go any further."

"Someone might steal them," said Dan.

Vel made a show of looking around at the empty land around them.

"Vel," Caid said, "I sense you're nervous about what we're about do to, and I'm curious as to the cause."

"I can guess the cause," Alice said. "It's got something to do with the Depot." A bolt of surprise widened her eyes. "Wait! And something to do with the Alliance, yeah?"

Vel's didn't answer directly. Instead, she said, "Captain, are you open to mistrusting the Depot?"

"Susy, dear, I'm open to mistrusting *anyone* if it justifies getting into a little trouble."

Vel turned to Dan. "What about you?"

He appeared frozen solid. Then, miraculously, he swallowed and nodded.

"The comms are off, Dan. They can't hear you speak anymore. Whatever. Caid? Are you open to mistrusting them?"

"Absolutely."

Alice snapped her head around to face him. "Whoa. Where'd *that* come from? Aren't you Mr. Touchy Feely? Don't you think everyone's misunderstood and deserves a second chance?"

Caid pressed his palms together and bowed slightly. "It's fascinating to hear your view of me, Alice. Thank you for sharing that gift. But some people, some organizations in this case, cannot be trusted. Yes, those people probably came from broken homes and lack a secure attachment in their lives. They probably never experienced trustworthiness from those around them in early childhood and missed out on unconditional love. Doesn't change the fact that some people are so deep in their own pain that they cannot be trusted to consider the well-being of others in their decisions. Or rather, they can be trusted only to be untrustworthy. Take, for instance, everyone we've encountered on this planet. I can love them and understand why they are the way they are, but I don't choose to invite unhealthy behaviors and intentions into my own life."

Alice cupped her hands over her mouth and nose. "Oh

my god, I didn't think I could be this bored." She tilted her head back, groaning. "Caid, my guy, can you just answer the damn question?"

"I thought I was."

"Nooo, the one about why you're suddenly ready to drop the Depot like a cold-hearted gangster after all they've done for you."

"I've spoken with all of the crew members on these missions. At first, it was as the crew's diplomat, as a mental health professional. Always as a friend. People tell me things. Lots of things. Just because I've sworn an oath not to tell anyone what they say, including my employer, doesn't mean I *forget* what I hear."

"Whoa, Nelly," Alice said. "There's a lot to mine there. Can you tell us what the crew members told you before you were their therapist?"

Caid chuckled. "Oh, Alice. I might not have been a therapist, but I was still a trusted friend. I wouldn't dream of sharing what they told me with others, like I wouldn't dream of sharing what you've told me with others."

Alice shook her head, wondering why she was still engaging with him on the topic.

They finished hiding their comms in one of the stationary bushes, hoping the thing didn't manage to ingest the equipment, then Vel pointed at something ahead, which Alice had mistaken for a shriveled toadstool. It wasn't.

It was a wooden sign.

It read, *This way is dull. Nothing to see.*

"*Phew,*" said Dan. "Okay, I can do dull."

Vel continued onward.

Around the bend of the large red hill, they came upon another sign: *Sweet VOID, this way is boring. You should turn back around now.*

It was a curious thing for a sign to say, Alice concluded. No, not curious, suspicious. And Vel seemed to take it as confirmation that they were, in fact, on the right path.

The next sign simply said, *WARNING: RISK OF DYING OF BOREDOM AHEAD.*

"Susy? Maybe we should listen to it. I was always afraid that's how I'd go."

"I assure you, you're at no risk of it, Captain."

And then finally, as they reached the mouth of a dark cave, one final sign: *YOU KNOW WHAT? GO AHEAD. WE WARNED YOU AND YOU DIDN'T LISTEN. GO AHEAD AND DIE OF BOREDOM FROM THE ABSOLUTE LACK OF THINGS TO SEE INSIDE THIS DULL-ASS CAVE.*

"Wow," Dan said, "I've never wanted to enter a cave more. Sounds excellent."

"You puzzle me," Alice said, staring at the minister. "How does someone who wants to play the chimney game on Britannica also want to enter the multiverse's most boring cave?"

Dan grinned. "I'm a complicated guy."

Caid leaned toward the captain. "Dysregulated nervous system."

"I'm glad you're ready, Dan," said Vel. "Because we're going in." She reached into her jumpsuit pocket and pulled out the emergency light stick, shaking it to agitate the tiny plankton inside. Once they were angrily aglow, she led the way in. "Shouldn't be far," she said. "I'm guessing it'll be obvious."

No one bothered asking *what* would be obvious.

Alice entered the cave and found herself completely swallowed up by darkness, not even a pinprick of light behind her now.

And then she entered the cave.

"Huh?" She could've sworn she'd *already* entered the cave a moment before. She looked at Dan on her left, who appeared equally surprised by the development.

"Shouldn't be far," Vel said. "I'm guessing it'll be obvious." She pulled up short. "Wait, did I already say that?"

Alice entered the cave and found herself completely surrounded by darkness, not even a pinprick of light behind her now, only finding her way by the glow of Vel's light stick.

Again? Did I enter again? Or maybe the first couple of times were … my imagination?

Remembering she had her own glow stick, she pulled it out and shook it. Dan quickly did the same. "History," Dan said softly. "I suspect it's been rewritten too many times in this place."

"Shouldn't be far," Vel said. Then, "Blast! I said it again, didn't I?"

"Ghasselite?" Alice asked.

"Does it feel like Ghasselite?" Dan replied.

She considered it. "No. It's more like the dizziness when we entered the containment barrier. The arrow of time issue."

He hopped, pulling a quick one-eighty to make sure no one was sneaking up behind him. All clear. "But it feels much stronger here."

Alice entered the cave and found herself completely surrounded by darkness, not even a pinprick—

Son of a bitch.

She pulled her light stick out of her jumpsuit again and shook it. Again.

Ahead of her, Vel gasped and stopped in her tracks.

Alice hurried over to see what the lieutenant's light had

fallen upon. "Sweet baby …"

Alice entered the cave and found herself completely surrounded by darkness—

Fuck me.

She jogged to catch up with Vel again, tripped, remembered she hadn't shaken her light stick yet, shook it, and then caught up to the lieutenant in time for Vel to stop in her tracks and gasp, and for Alice, yet again, to spot the reason for their side trip. "Sweet baby Jesus."

Dan reached them and pulled up short, drawing a very large blaster and aiming it ahead on instinct. His dysregulated nervous system was all out of flight, freeze, fawn, and flop. He put his finger on the trigger.

"What am I looking at, Susy?"

Vel shook her head. "They said it would be here, but I had no idea it would be this bad."

A deep, tragic wail rose up behind them, and Alice turned to see Caid, his natural soft glow negating the need for a light stick. He stumbled past them, arms in the air, and made it down the embankment into the small crater below, making for the nearest visible victim.

Alice entered the cave and found herself—

Fuck, fuck, shit.

She shook her light stick impatiently and rushed forward again. Caid was already down in the crater, trying his best to hug one of the bodies. The blue jumpsuit, the very same style as her own, gave away the significance of this find even before she noticed the Depot's insignia on the breast.

The scene around her was tragic—four lost souls, condemned to spend the rest of their lives and then eternity in this time-fluttering hell.

Caid hugged one who slightly resembled a bagpipe, but now wasn't the time to fixate on that. Two of the bagpipe's drones were shackled to the cave wall, keeping the long-dead victim unable to lie down and find some peace.

Alice knelt by Caid, trying to focus on anything other than his tearful whimpers and inability to hold the body despite his trying. "Who were they?"

"My first crew. My very first crew! Djaar! Marifa! Svat'palnka! Terry!"

It was only the last word that tipped off Alice to the fact that Caid was wailing the names of the lost and not speaking in some foreign grief language. She raised her light stick to extend the radius of its glow over this morbid indentation in the ground.

No, not an indentation, but a prison cell. A death chamber. The previous crew members were strung up around the place, in hardly a state of decay at all. Then Alice felt a quick shudder in the air and they were all bones, jumpsuits in bunches below them. Another shudder, then back to the fleshy, preserved bodies. Alice shivered and made a promise to herself to never rewrite history.

"Djaar! Marifa! Svat'palnka! Terry!"

She thought, *Damn, it happened again,* before realizing, no, this bit of grief was fresh. Caid was wailing their names a second time. Grief in its deepest form wasn't one and done. It repeated, came back fresh. It moved along its own arrow; it lived on a separate timeline.

She got to her feet, hoping to whomever that she didn't have to enter this cave again, and looked back at Vel and Dan, who had remained on the edge of the depression. As the captain, she ought to know what to do here, but all she *wanted* to do was put this out of her mind as quickly as possible, and that didn't seem like the leaderly thing to do.

Since there was no dragging Caid away from the bodies even if she'd wanted to, she was left with no choice but to give him the time and space he needed, and while he did that, she climbed back out from the crater. Putting her back to the scene gave her the heebie-jeebies, and she scrambled, felt herself sliding back, and reached out for a hand. Vel caught it in her firm grip and pulled her the rest of the way out.

"Question," Alice said. "What the hell is this, Susy? I mean, seriously. How did you know about this place, and why did you bring us?"

She entered the cave and found herself completely surrounded by darkness.

"Fuck's sake." She shook her light stick and jogged over to Vel again. She seemed to be the only one who had experienced a reset.

"The Alliance tipped me off to it," Vel said, staring down at Caid and oblivious to Alice's disappearance and reappearance beside her. "Astra Blum said if I was so certain we were on the right side by working for the Depot, I should find this place. She said it's the kind of fate DeepService Team Ones meet when the Depot has no more use for them, assuming something else doesn't kill them first."

Dan gagged on his own saliva. His subsequent cough rang out through the space. "I'm sorry, but when you say 'done with them,' might that apply to when a crew decides to … abandon the mission?"

"Now hold up," Alice said. "Astra could've been making that all up. Just because she led you to this place, Susy, doesn't mean anything. For all we know, the *Alliance* did this to these people. That'd explain how they knew where to lead you, wouldn't it?"

Vel paused. "I guess."

"And why would the Alliance, who tried to assassinate us

not once but twice and who lieutenantnapped you, tell you anything like this anyway? What's it to them if we find this mess down here? Look at what it's doing to Caid! Ever thought they only wanted to hurt him and scare us?"

"It felt more like a warning, Captain."

"A warning of what *they* have planned if they can ever get ahold of us? Huh?"

"They said many of them were DeepService Team One once, too."

Alice wanted to call bullshit, but something in Vel's face stopped her. "The cactus guy? He was on a DeepService crew?"

"No, I don't think so. Astra said he used to run a small business, remember? He joined up after the Depot crushed his business. Why do you care about him?"

"Nothing. He's just weird. You know his arm grew back? Goddamn gecko shit."

Caid scaled the side of the crater with ease enough, but slowly, his arms began hanging limply by his side, his energy spent. His glow was faint. "I didn't know," he said. "I didn't know what happened to them. I thought …" More holographic tears came, along with shameless, full-bellied sobbing that Alice didn't think she could muster herself if she'd tried.

"I'd gone on a mission independently," he managed between sobs, "since I was at no risk myself. We'd split up. They went to the city, and I met with a private company."

"Here?" Alice asked, trying to make sense of Caid's incoherent confession.

"Not here. It was somewhere else. We were supposed to meet back at the ship, and they never did. Their comms cut out. They never came back … they never came back." He gasped, despite not needing air. "I waited for them to arrive at the rendezvous spot until the Depot told me to come back on my own. They—the crew had discussed abandoning their mission and making a break for it, and in my heart I'd hoped that was what happened, that they got away, that they escaped." He shook his head miserably.

Vel was the one to initiate, holding out her arms, tapping Dan and Alice on the shoulders to get them onboard. And then the three shipmates came together around Caid in a group hug, encircling the space he took up. It was all they could do.

But as Alice continued pretending she could feel the hologram and reminded herself not to get worked up thinking about pressing her body against his, she caught a glimpse of a yellow jumpsuit in her periphery—a remnant of a Depot crew that had considered abandoning their mission —and felt a deep dread run through her.

The morale on *Emergence* had seen better days. Once boarded, Vel took the replacement part and marched wordlessly to the machine room to allow Allura to tell her exactly where to put it.

That left Dan, Alice, and Caid on the bridge, but only momentarily, as Caid sniffled hugged himself tightly, then hurried out on a heaving sob, heading for his chambers.

"Allura. Beer."

"Coming right up, Daddy."

Alice grabbed the bottle from the kitchenette slot and plopped down into one of the nearby chairs at the table, trying to ignore Dan as he paced the length of the bridge.

The minister of weapons and culture rubbed at the back of his neck and glared at the floor ahead of him, as if it might give up the goods. "We can still try to make things right with Emperor Best," he said. "It'll be hard, but—"

"Not hard, Dan. Impossible. Can you honestly imagine a scenario where he accepts *any* apology from me?"

"We could still try. And maybe we could also track down Aubert Orleans and tell him we were kidding. Oh!

Better yet, we could tell Liz Windsor that he was lying about our firing him as a client. Maybe the comms didn't pick up the interaction. The market was noisy. I bet she'd believe us if we stuck to our story. We could still make this right."

Alice let her head fall into her hands. "No, we can't."

"We have to! Why wouldn't we at least try?"

She rocked her head back, staring up at the bright lights, wishing one would suck her particles up into it and transport her somewhere—anywhere—else. "Even if we made things right with Aubert—which, ew—we would still face the problem of finding a match for the Yoken."

"There's gotta be another planet as bad as Trauna."

"I'm sure there is somewhere in this godforsaken star cluster. But do you think breeding the two psychotic species together will solve that ol' infanticide problem?"

"That's not what we were paid to do. We're here to make babies, not protect—"

"Whoa, whoa, whoa. I'm gonna do you a *huge* favor and keep you from finishing that sentence. I know you're, like, freaking out, but you really gotta up your standards of who you buddy up with. The Yoken ain't it."

Dan didn't have an answer to that and paused in his pacing. Then he resumed, "There has to be another option."

"And what if there isn't?" she snapped. "What if there is no way out? What if we're *trapped*? What if we're trapped forever and there's no escaping this?!" She hurriedly chugged her beer, hoping he didn't catch the desperation in her voice.

But he did. His open-mouthed gaping made that clear. "Are you saying you don't know the next step?"

"I know the next step," she said irritably. "It's finishing this beer. I might even know the next two steps: finishing this beer and opening another. Look at Alice! She's thinking so far ahead now!"

Dan dropped into the chair opposite her. "Could it be true, though? Do you think the Depot might've chained up that crew back there?"

"I don't know what to think, and thinking is not really the vibe I'm going for right now. Not after that." She shuddered, as a wave of panic washed over her that she could, at any moment, find herself entering that cave again as the darkness surrounded her. "Could've been the Depot," she said, trying to distract herself, "could've been the Alliance. What are either of them to us? Can't trust 'em farther than you can spit."

"Then who *can* be trusted?" There was a plea to his question that indicated she should be careful with her next words, that he was teetering on the edge of an internal crisis and her answer could nudge him one way or the other.

"Hell if I know." She stood. "I think it's high time I take Caid up on all those desperate offers of therapy."

She left Dan on the bridge and made the short trip down the hall to Caid's room. But it was fruitless, as she should have known. When he answered the door, he only opened it a crack. "Yes?"

"I think I need to talk."

"I'm sorry," he said, "I can't hold that emotional space for you right now. I need time to myself to process this trauma." And then he shut the door in her face.

Great. Now what? She couldn't return to the bridge and face Dan and his incessant questions, and Vel was still busy working on the ship so they could get the hell off this planet and out of the containment field as fast as humanly possible. That left her all to herself.

Well, there was Allura, who could be in multiple places

at once within the operating system—both helping Vel install the part and speaking with Alice—but for some strange reason, Alice didn't think being called Daddy would do much for her.

Man, I'm really in a tizzy, ain't I?

She returned to her quarters, and as soon as she closed the door, she felt it settle in. That blanket. Smothering, weighted, possibly never-ending. Once she was under it, she was certain she'd never escape, but in that moment, there was no escaping if she'd tried.

She flopped facedown onto her bed and felt the blanket lower over her, press her to the mattress. It was almost nice to give in. This was all her fault anyway, when it came down to it. Maybe if she'd bothered to think more than one step ahead, she could've found some other route for them much, much earlier in this assignment. Maybe they never would've entered Star Cluster B, never would've wrecked this ship, never would've found those bodies. Caid would still be in good spirits, Dan would be back to his old self, and Vel …

Vel would still be moody.

She'd been holding all of that in this whole time. That doubt about the Depot, about their responsibility working for the conglomerate. It was out now, a contagious thing, and Vel's doubts had become Alice's as well.

You did it again, idiot. People relied on you, and you screwed them all over. You lost your temper on the emperor and now you're all dead.

The one thing she'd hoped this job could provide her, a means of escape from the life she'd accidentally built for herself, the trap she'd ensnared herself in, had turned out to be yet another broken promise. There was no escape anywhere in the multiverse.

With each pulsing in her temples, her brain taunted her with *trapped, trapped, trapped.*

The stifling blanket of pain pressed her harder to the bed, adding unbearable weight to her limbs, making her internal organs feel heavy even as every cell in her body vibrated with a compressed desire to run. And there she hovered, potential energy trapped within her, unable to move, Dan's unanswered question echoing in her skull: Who could she trust? Certainly not herself.

Alice Luck couldn't be sure how long she'd remained motionless, facedown on her bed, feeling like the universe was contracting around her. It could have been an hour, could have been three days. Time, as she was learning, was a buncha bull.

According to the clock on her wall, however, she'd been lying there for eight minutes and twenty-nine seconds.

A knock at the door put an end to her motionlessness, and she moaned at the thought of getting up. The weight was still heavy on her, and though it threatened to crush her to death, it was also quite *snuggly.*

She rolled onto her side and stared at the door, as if that might be enough to end this situation.

But another knock confirmed that staring at doors did not solve problems.

Alice groaned then regretted that no one could hear her do so, because it was quite a dramatic one that displayed how put out she was by all this, and then she rolled off the bed and answered the door.

"I'm sorry" were the first words out of Vel's mouth as she stood there. "Maybe I should have told you everything that happened between me and the Alliance sooner, but I don't know that I could have."

"It's fine."

"You're just saying that."

"No, really, it's fine."

"You're lying. You don't take apologies well."

"Psh. Like you have me figured out. Please. Come inside so no one can hear you pouring your heart out to me."

Vel stepped inside Alice's chambers but stood her ground hardly a yard inside the door. "I didn't think you'd believe any of it."

The captain folded her arms over her chest. "Why'd you think that?"

"Because I didn't fully believe any of it. Why would I expect you to do something I couldn't?"

"I can do plenty of things you can't."

"Like?"

Alice grunted, rolling her head. "Can we stay on topic? You came to apologize for being wrong."

"It seemed likely that they were lying, so I had to verify it for myself."

"That's why you recommended we go to Trauna, isn't it?"

"It is." Vel swallowed hard. "I'm sorry. I knew it was dangerous, and we could have crash-landed in a way that kept us from ever leaving without an extraction ... which I'm starting to believe might not have happened. I understand if I've lost your trust, Captain, but I do intend to gain it back over time through reliable action."

Alice had always been able to spot the parts of Vel that were hardened by war and fighting. Those were easy enough to see. The stony brows, the boxy jaw from gritting teeth, not to mention the actual scars—three angry slashes above the lieutenant's collarbone that peeked out above the neckline of her jumpsuit like they were checking to make sure the coast was clear.

What Alice couldn't have known was that these scars were from long before Vel had seen any action—she'd tried to domesticate a particularly aggressive tomcat in her youth, and he'd wanted none of it.

But what Alice noticed for the first time now were the soft parts of Vel—the parentheses around her mouth, her tired shoulders, that she picked at one of her cuticles with her thumbnail while her hands were balled up into fists.

"Come here," Alice said. "I want to show you something."

She led Vel into the lab, and when she got onto her knees, Vel didn't immediately follow form.

"What is—"

Alice held her finger to her lips then slipped under the table, only barely noticing the much reduced pain in her arm when it brushed the floor. She motioned for Vel to join her.

"Did you—" But Alice scooted out again and slapped a hand over Vel's mouth.

"Stay here."

She returned a moment later with the radical redshift marker from her bedside table, a tool that a different captain might've used to do calculations or jot down action plans. So far, she'd only used it to write, *ALICE'S LAB, BITCHES!* on the laboratory's whiteboard along with a fancy S she'd learned to draw in middle school.

It hadn't clicked at the time of writing that she was using a permanent marker on the whiteboard, and so the writing remained there.

But now she was putting it to a more conspiratorial purpose for the marker.

This time, when she slid underneath the table, Vel joined her.

Alice wrote *look* on the bottom of the table and drew an arrow from her word to the existing ones.

Vel cast a curious glance her captain's way.

Alice wrote, *Dead zone? No surv—* and wished she knew how to spell *surveillance*. She scribbled over the last two words and wrote instead: *Depot cannot detect.*

Vel shook her head, her eyes wide, then she held up a finger. She slipped out from under the table and returned a moment later with a dry-erase marker from the board. She scribbled it over the permanent marker then wiped away both with her wrist.

"Whoa," Alice said. "I had no idea you could do that."

Vel snatched the radical redshift marker from her captain and wrote, *It's the color.*

Alice mouthed, "What?"

Marker color, Vel wrote. *Only humans can see it.*

Alice grabbed it back and scribbled, *How do you know?*

The marker traded hands again. *Everybody knows. Why do you have it if you don't know?*

Alice whispered, "It's pretty."

Vel rolled her eyes, erased their recent writing, then wrote, *Star Cluster A?* She gestured at the original words Alice had brought her down there to see.

Alice took the marker back. *You know about it?*

Vel shook her head. *Who wrote?*

Alice replied: *Old cap?*

Vel: *What does it mean?*

Alice: *No clue. Reminds me of your thing tho.*

Vel: *Same. What do we do now?*

Alice: *Speak to Liz Windsor?*

Vel: *Seems risky.*

Alice: *I love risky.*

Vel chuckled.

Alice grabbed the marker one last time, drew a simplified version of a human male's reproductive organs, and labeled it *Star Cluster D*.

Let the next crew figure *that* out.

CHAPTER
TWENTY-ONE

Back on the bridge, as *Emergence* managed to sneak out of the containment field, unnoticed this time, the bridge comms signaled a call, which Alice had expected they would. A moment later, the front window went partially opaque, and the face of Liz Windsor appeared before them.

The whole crew had gathered for liftoff, and the ship was feeling much more spacious now that their client cargo had been offloaded.

"I've just had the strangest call with Aubert Orleans."

"Hi, Liz Windsor." Alice waved. "Thanks for letting us out of that containment field. How are you doing on this fine ... whatever day it is for you back on Blerg VFP69?"

The liaison acted as if Alice hadn't spoken at all. "He said that you attempted to fire him and then left him on his home planet. I see he's not with you now. I'm quite confused. You couldn't have possibly fired someone as nice as Aubert without just cause, of which I'm sure none exists. So, I suppose I'm curious where the miscommunication occurred that led him to believe the Depot had dropped him as a client."

"The only misunderstanding I see here," Alice said, "is that he told you we 'attempted' to fire him. I *straight up* fired his ass, along with all the asses and ass-like parts on Trauna. Liz Windsor, you know you're my girl, you know I love you, but what in the batwinged fuck was the Depot thinking bringing him on as a client? *You* might be under some contractual obligation to speak kindly of him, but you weren't born yesterday." She cringed, remembering that the liaison might not be totally organic, and therefore being born could be a touchy subject. "You know as well as we do that Aubert Orleans was obnoxious as all get out, and that's to say it gently. We met with Emperor Best, and that lunatic was even worse. And now, you might be saying, 'That's two men on an entire planet,' but I can assure you, we mingled with the locals. It's *everyone*. They're all meaner than a feral hog in heat."

Liz Windsor blinked and nodded so minutely that Alice wondered if it'd even happened. Either way, the captain was under the distinct impression that the liaison's slow reaction had less to do with any lag in communications and more to do with having her attention split. Was she receiving some kind of instructions?

Just as well. Alice didn't know how any of this intergalactic tech worked, but she was raised to know that nothing she said on the internet would stay private, and this was a little like that. Someone else was listening in, she was sure of it.

"I won't tell you you're wrong, Captain Luck—"

"Good, because we were recently stumbling around whole heaps of ghasselite, and I'm not in the mood."

"—but I will say this: we are well aware of the situation with Trauna and the behavior of its people, especially the

Yoken. However, have you considered that we were attempting to *neutralize* the situation so that, generations from now, they could begin to lead happy lives and possibly leave the containment zone? We were hoping you might find a good-natured population they could pair with, one that would smooth the hard edges and infuse the gene pool with some hereditary empathy."

Alice put her hands on her hips. "What cuckoo world are y'all living in? Those folks are monsters. Pairing them with a gentle population is like throwing a fuzzy rabbit into an anaconda's cage because the snake seems lonely. No, Liz Windsor, we spoke with the emperor about their reproductive issues, and it's a whole bag of crazy. They rape. That's it. That's how they reproduce. And I know that as a human I don't have much ground to stand on in judging them, since my people have been known to love a good rapin' too. But that's all they do on Trauna. Then they force the women—who are victims, certainly, but also more unhinged than a possum neck-deep in a meth stash—to carry the babies to term. Then once the baby's out, these psychos leave it wherever it falls and see if it survives. I mean, Liz Windsor, what the hell *is* that?"

"Some might call that 'survival of the fittest.'"

"Decent folks would call it 'twenty-five to life.'"

Liz Windsor turned her giant head toward Dan, who stood silently with the rest of the crew behind the captain. "Minister Zone, maybe you can help impress upon Captain Luck that we may not understand every culture, but we can still accept that they might do things a little differently from what would be considered appropriate within our native society."

"Please," Alice said before Dan could respond. "I like

you, Liz Windsor, so I hope you'll spare me that nonsense. They call sex 'walloping.' You know why? Because the males beat a woman—"

"Or intersex," Vel added.

"—or intersex person into submission so they can do it to her. Them."

Even Liz Windsor couldn't resist a look of distaste at that. Alice seized the momentum and went on. "You hired me because of my knowledge in animal husbandry. Well, I gotta tell you, if any bull or turkey or prize hog acted this way, we'd take it to the slaughterhouse, not *breed* it."

"Are you suggesting we kill everyone on Trauna and be done with them?"

"What? God no! No, no, no. I would never say to kill off an entire planet. Those walking shrub things seemed pretty chill. I'm sure there are a few other life forms that aren't as bad. And I'm also sure the Yoken are finding ways to assault them all. No, I'm not gonna say killing is the answer, but *if*, say, a single planet *had* to go for whatever reason—yeah, I know which one I'd pick."

After another long pause, Liz Windsor continued. "Very well. You make a strong case, one I'll run up the chain of command. In the meantime, since it's clear to me that this particular assignment is at an impasse, I'm officially marking it as a failed mission. That will go on the crew's record." She sighed. "I had hoped it wouldn't come to this. The team had so much promise."

Alice and Vel shared a concerned look.

"I'm programming *Emergence* to head back to Blerg VFP69," Liz Windsor continued. "Once you've arrived, I'll let you know what we've decided."

"Decided about what?" Alice asked.

"Have a pleasant trip back home, Captain Luck. And to the rest of you, I look forward to seeing you shortly."

"Decided about what?" Alice repeated.

The liaison's face disappeared, and the bridge remained silent within the vacuum of space. The stars appeared to move around them as the ship changed directions at Liz Windsor's command and began its route back to Blerg VFP69, known to the locals as Earth.

Dan broke the silence. "They're gonna kill us, aren't they?"

Alice let her hands fall from her hips. "They can try. But if we can survive Trauna and Britannica, I think we'll be all right."

Lordy, how she wished she had a clue what was going on. Too many disturbing bits of information, too many claims, swirled around in her mind.

She turned her attention to the other three beings on her crew. She could trust them. But was there anyone else she could trust?

"Caid," she said, "what's the confidentiality situation with your sessions and the Depot? Do they have access to the records?"

He gasped. "I would *never* let that happen. My entire cabin has been equipped so that no records of anything happening inside it can be accessed by anyone but me. I keep my own records, of course, but they're not connected to the main system in any way."

Alice massaged the crick in her neck from having spent so much time under the laboratory table. "You sure?"

"Positive," said Caid. "I can sense the frequencies of their surveillance technology. They are not connected to my records."

Alice rolled her shoulders back. "Okay, then. I think it's time we have a group therapy session."

The hologram's eyes glowed, literally. "I thought you'd never ask."

CHAPTER
TWENTY-TWO

To create a relaxing environment for the most reluctant member of the crew to engage in therapy, Caid set up his room to believably resemble an overgrown pasture. Nestled within the tall growth was a dirt patch with four overturned logs (three substantial, one holographic) surrounding a crackling firepit. It was night out, the star patterns above mimicking those found on Blerg VFP69 on June twenty-fifth, two thousand and ten years after the birth year of a mythic man, which was not quite his actual birth year, since nobody had thought to write that down at the time.

Despite having been the one to initiate this group session and the nostalgic bonfire in front of her, Captain Alice Luck exhibited all the body language of someone clamming up tight. She had her feet kicked out in front of her with her arms crossed over her chest, shoulders hunched. Caid logged that in his mental notes.

"Are we secure?" Dan asked. "Can you assure us that everything we say for the duration of the session will stay between us?"

"Yes, so long as you're in here and we keep Allura out, we should maintain confidentiality."

"I don't like that," Alice said. "Allura should be allowed in. She's part of the crew, and we already know she saved our ass more than once. If we ask her not to relay information back to headquarters, she'll comply. It's a kink of hers."

"She's the onboard operating system," Vel said firmly. "Her whole job is to operate a Depot craft and relay its information back to the Depot."

"You're selling her short here, Susy. She's so much more than that. I can tell."

"Fill her in later, then, Captain," Dan said. "That's your prerogative. It will likely get us all killed, but you're in charge."

Caid tried not to show his excitement at this interesting development. "That's her prerogative?"

But before Dan could elaborate, Alice leaned forward, waving her hands to cut through anything emotional that was brewing. "Knock it off, Caid. We're not here to talk about our feelings. We have some questions that need answering. Dan clearly thinks the Depot is bringing us back to dispose of us. Caid, you might have other theories after your, uh …"

"Trauma," he supplied. "You can speak its name."

"Fine. The point is that y'all have theories, but I can't even formulate one of those because I have no *fucking* clue what's happening in this multiverse. I lack context. For instance, has anyone heard of something called Star Cluster A?"

Alice looked first to Caid, and while something about it poked at an old memory, he had nothing of use to supply and shook his head.

Dan also came up empty. "I think I would've heard of that if it existed."

"Would you?" Alice asked. "You've been working for the Man most of your career."

"The Ministry of Weapons and Culture is technically a neutral institution with a clear mission statement of—"

"Yeah, I know it: *All hail the Man.*"

Vel jumped in. "Captain Luck found something in her lab. She showed me a little while ago. It was written on the bottom of one of the metal tables in a color only visible to the human eye." As she continued to describe it and their assumptions around it, Caid's mind ran through the previous crew members he knew who would have had unfettered access to that equipment. It wasn't many. Ten, perhaps. If he narrowed it down to the humans, only four. Which one of them might've written that in there, and could it mean something other than what Alice was implying?

"Supply count," Dan said. "Maybe that's what the SC means. Maybe someone was doing inventory."

"*Inventory?*" Alice asked incredulously. "What, and they couldn't find their tablet, so they wrote it on the bottom of the table along with the words *do not play their game*? What, the game of *stocking samples*?"

"It's hard to deny the meaning of SC-A," Caid said, letting his professionalism drop as his conspiracy theories took root. He knew such ideas were a product of an imbalanced mind, but in this case, perhaps not. He *had* seen quite a few crews come and go, and he'd never heard from any of them again. Could they all have met the fate of Djaar, Marifa, Svat'palnka, and Terry? After being assigned a client like Aubert Orleans, the mission had stretched his loyalty and rational thinking to its bounds. He didn't want to lose yet another group of friends.

"The existence of Star Cluster B implies a Star Cluster A," Vel added. "I don't think we ought to function under any other assumption."

Dan began nodding, slowly at first, but then more adamantly. "Maybe it was something that existed before the Great War."

Alice arched a brow at him. "Which one was that? Civil War or WWII?"

"Neither. I'm not talking about piddly Earth wars. I'm talking about *the* Great War. The one that ravaged the universe and allowed the Depot to take over."

Alice narrowed her eyes at him. "See, this is what I'm talking about. I don't know jack about any of this."

Dan fidgeted on his log, trying to contain his excitement. "Sheesh, where do I start? The Great War? Wow. Um … Okay. So, ever since intelligent life began forming approximately thirteen billion years ago, things were pretty violent."

"The creation of this iteration of the universe was extremely traumatic for everyone," Caid added.

"Right. And things remained hot and traumatic even as races began launching themselves into the cosmos. Usually, it was little scrapes between neighboring planets—a swift genocide, something simple like that—but as with all things in existence, a few of these skirmishes began to grow and escalate.

"Two small conflicts attracted each other and folded into one larger conflict. Then that conflict folded into another conflict and so on, growing larger and larger."

"Not every conflict added on, though," Caid added. "Some fizzled out. And it should be said that many races, despite their shared trauma of existence, *did not* choose to express their pain through warfare."

"Sure, fine," Dan said, "but they got swept up in it anyway, didn't they? The conflict grew to be too large, too messy. Galaxy after galaxy became a war zone. Then those galaxies began to ally with other galaxies until almost all of our universe was engaged in battle. It wasn't even clear what either side wanted, other than to destroy the other."

"*Other* being the key word," Caid said. "There can be no war without othering."

"Caid, nobody knows what you're talking about," Alice said. "Keep going, Dan. The war stuff has my interest."

"The height of the war was chaos. Entire battalions got confused about who they were aligned with and attacked their allies by mistake. Among the Great War, mini squabbles broke out, turning the universe into a frantic tangle of firepower.

"It was the perfect landscape for a neutral peacemaking party to arrive on scene and be warmly received. And that's what the Depot did. They came from a part of the universe that had been off-limits to the war, one so weak, so underdeveloped, so dull, and yet so inexplicably vicious that neither side of the conflict had any interest in aligning with it. It's what you know as the Milky Way galaxy. The rest of the universe knew it as ... Well, at that point, there were still various dominant languages, which obviously contributed to a lot of the miscommunications, but if you were to translate the most common languages into English, you would get a name that is essentially the Poison Death Trash Galaxy. *Roughly* that."

Alice cringed. "Never feels good to know people are talking about you behind your back."

"Don't worry," Dan said, "because the Depot changed

that perception when they intervened in the war. Now, as you've seen, the Depot is held in the highest esteem throughout the universe. They saved an entire *universe* from itself. Haven't you noticed that that little patch on your jumpsuit can get us access almost anywhere?"

"I didn't think it was possible," Alice said, "but you're making me feel a *little* better about the job. Thanks. I don't mind being on the side of the peacemakers."

"Exactly!" Dan waggled a finger at her, lost in the thrill of finally having someone to use his war knowledge on. "Nobody does. The Depot came in and orchestrated the greatest peace accords this universe has ever seen. They were a virtually unknown force before it, and then after, everything changed. The Intergalactic Council was able to exist. Instead of fighting each other, planets began trading goods. All the languages became standardized to avoid further miscommunications, and it was voted that English, the language of the Depot itself, would be adopted universally. Admittedly, it was one of the more complicated languages to learn, but we're generations in on that, and most children are raised with it now. Another result of the peace is that Blerg VFP69, the original home of the Depot, is held in the highest regard. Prior to the Depot's efforts, there was no way your planet would've earned the distinction of VFP. No way at all."

The group therapy session fell quiet as the only sound became the crackle of the fire between them.

Alice chewed on her lip, staring into the flames. "Are we on the right side, then? Are we the good guys, since we work for the Depot?"

"It's why I agreed to work *with* them and then eventually *for* them," Dan said.

Caid pressed his palms together and bowed slightly.

"Thank you for sharing that, Dan. It's always good to have a historical reminder." He chuckled. "I'll admit, my mind was spinning some real doozies about the Depot. Conspiracy theories galore! I forgot that this is the same conglomerate that saved the universe when it didn't have to."

"Hold up," Vel said. "Before we get all sentimental about Dear Daddy Depot, let us not forget about the bodies we discovered in that cave. Something is off here, period."

"I agree," Dan said. "But we don't know that what's off has anything to do with the Depot. Who told you where to find the bodies, Vel? Perhaps *they* were the ones who'd left them there."

"*They* were the Alliance members who kidnapped me, and *they were* part of a DeepService Team One!" Vel snapped. "We've been over this!"

Caid's heart, which didn't exist except in metaphor, nearly stopped. "What did you just say?"

"Not *all* of them were DeepService, but their leader, Astra, was before she abandoned the Depot and joined the Alliance."

"What if the Depot *is* the bad guy?" Alice said. "Just supposing," she added to Vel. "I'm not entirely there yet. But just supposing the Depot is the bad guy, what about that?"

"How would they be the bad guy?" Dan asked. "They saved the universe from itself. They're still the only thing maintaining the peace."

"And that gives them an awful lot of power," Alice added. "You know, where I come from, we ain't big on outsiders telling us what to do, especially when they're telling us what's best for us. How come the Depot gets to be the peacemaker? How come they *still* get to call the shots?"

Vel had an answer for that. "My universe went through something similar."

"Of course it did," Dan said. "It's parallel."

"Yeah, but it wasn't *exactly* the same. I suspect we were a few thousand years ahead of your universe, whatever time's worth between universes. We had the same intergalactic war, and we had a single so-called neutral entity come in to broker peace. And because of that, they were put in charge. And then terror reigned for a thousand years, only it was under a single ruling group rather than multiple warring factions."

Lines of concern appeared around Dan's almond eyes. "And then what happened?"

Vel shrugged. "I don't know. By the time I left and came here, the terror was still terrorizing."

"And you fought in those conflicts?" Alice asked. "Or, wait, you're not a thousand years old. But you fought. Who were you fighting for?"

"The Point. That's who was in charge. I was one of theirs. I helped enforce the peace."

"But you were a warrior."

"You can't ask people nicely to stop killing each other and expect it to happen."

"True," said Alice. "My middle school principal tried that once. Didn't work. He had to drag me off Caroline Turton kicking and screaming. In my defense, she blindsided me with a slap to the ear, and *damn* if that doesn't smart. I started swinging. Didn't even know who I was fighting until Principal Peters pulled me free."

"Yes," Vel said dryly, "what I'm talking about is *just* like that."

"It sounds," Caid began, "like we're split on where everyone's trust lies. Vel, it sounds like you're leaning toward mistrust of the Depot." The lieutenant confirmed his suspicion with a nod. "And Dan, it sounds like you may question the current actions of the Depot that have brought us to this point in our mission, but you still believe strongly in the Depot's purpose."

"That about nails it," the minister of weapons and culture said.

"And Alice, it sounds like ..." Caid paused. "I'm not sure where you stand. Is that because you're not sure as well?"

"Damn skippy," said the captain. "I don't have a goddamn clue what's going on here. But I do know one thing: I trust the people in this room. Allura, too. And then that's it."

"What about Liz Windsor?" Caid said. "What are your feelings on her?"

Alice's eyes remained on the crackling fire as she spoke. "No idea. But I guess we'll find out about her soon enough, huh?"

CHAPTER
TWENTY-THREE

As the blue marble of Earth came into view from *Emergence*, Alice's thoughts went thus:

Wow, it looks like a marble.

I live on that marble.

I wonder how many of our astronauts have gotten it on in space.

I could really go for some pizza.

Then she remembered the virus, the one Liz Windsor told her about that had shut down the pizza places on Earth the last time she was there. Was it still spreading throughout that little marble? How much Earth time had passed while they'd been on their mission?

Ugh. The mission.

A pinprick of fear jabbed at her between her eyes every time she remembered. Had she done the wrong thing? Should she have stuck to playing the ugly game?

There was a strong chance the Depot would simply find another DeepService Team One to match the Yoken with an unsuspecting victim, and then Alice and her crew would be facing harsh consequences for, what, *integrity*? Since when had that gotten her anything but castigation, if not a full-fledged whoopin'?

Would the Depot give them all a whoopin'? The consequences for failing the trial mission had been clear enough: launched to the far reaches of the universe to die on a boring planet. While that possibility of punishment hadn't been mentioned prior to this mission, would a corporation who would do that to trainees really be more merciful to its employees?

Are they going to kill us?

No, that was too extreme. Except …

The cave. The goddamn cave.

Liz Windsor wouldn't execute that order, Alice was sure of it. The liaison wasn't the kind to do the dirty work, and Alice had a feeling she'd grown a soft spot for the crew. Which meant that someone else would have to do it, maybe even on a different planet. In that case, there would be ample opportunity for them to disappear if they had to. Hijack Allura's system, perhaps, and head to somewhere like Jaspariampt to live out their days in paradise.

See? She could think a few steps ahead when her life and happiness depended on it.

As the marble grew slowly in size, her mind drifted to the group therapy session. She hadn't intended it to be anything like therapy, but Caid had found a sneaky way to hijack it. Once the scheming was completed, he'd asked what everyone was most afraid of happening when they returned to the Depot headquarters.

Dan said: "That they'll fire us, and I'll never be able to find a job in my line of work again," Dan said.

Alice said: "That they'll fire us, and I'll be stuck on Earth for the rest of my life and have to, I dunno, pay taxes and sit in traffic."

Vel answered next. "That they'll tie us up in a cave somewhere, possibly torture us, and then leave us there to die." Those words laid one hell of a wet towel over an already soggy group. Alice hadn't truly considered being murdered as a possible option, despite what she'd seen in the cave. But after Vel's words, the thought was now lodged in her craw.

Hoping for a little optimism, Alice turned the question back on the asker. "What about you, Caid? What are you afraid will happen?"

"I don't have a specific scenario imagined, but I do worry that this crew will be disbanded, and I'll never see any of you again, one way or another. But I'll still be here, won't I? They can't physically kill me, so they're likely to keep me around. I'll still be here, and you all will be gone. That's my fear."

Alice thought that was the worst fear of them all. Always being left behind. Always the survivor. Forever and ever. Caid was facing a fate *worse* than death or taxes.

Not on my watch, you sexy air demon.

She would find a way to make this work. The important thing was not to think too hard about it ahead of time. That was the only superstition she held. Religion had never stuck for her, no matter how hard her mother shamed or her father hit, but *faith* had always made sense. Not faith in a grouchy buzzkill of a God who promised protection and, generally speaking, delivered destruction instead, but faith in *life*, in *the universe*. Her faith that the universe would provide what she needed when she needed it was as unshakeable as it was totally unfounded.

Liz Windsor would have no choice but to fire, at the very least, the captain of this ship. There was little Alice could do about that except keep her eyes and ears open in the moments leading up to it for some small morsel she might bite that could force the Depot, in all their anonymous power, to keep her around, to give her another chance that didn't involve an unmatchable client.

"Here we come," Allura said. "Buckle up. This is only going to hurt a little."

Alice secured herself into the captain's chair for entry into Earth's atmosphere. Flames danced in the center of the window, orange then red then purple. She curled her fingers around the armrest as the ship rattled. Earth, she was beginning to learn, fought more violently against intruders than most of the planets they'd visited. A sense of pride welled up in her.

The shaking stopped. The flames disappeared. They were hovering peacefully, miles above Earth, above her home, above everything she'd ever known prior to a few weeks ago. All her heartbreaks, all her pleasures, everyone she'd ever known previous to taking this job, existed on this peaceful blue speck in the greater multiverse. Despite the jeopardy she and her crew faced with the Depot, something warm and encouraging and familiar expanded inside her.

Before much longer, they were pulling into the Depot hangar. Everyone onboard noticed the gruff-looking guards waiting for them, but no one mentioned it.

The mood on the bridge was subdued as each member unbuckled then loaded onto the glass elevator down to the ship's cargo hangar. Vel flexed her hand next to her hip holster. For her, there was no fate worse than death. Death meant losing the fight for survival. She wouldn't lose. She wasn't a failure. She'd come too far. If she went out, she would go out fighting.

The two guards—one man and one woman, by the looks of it—stared expressionlessly through the port as it opened.

Oh yeah, Alice thought. *We're fucked.*

She paused in front of the male guard. "Your boot's untied."

His posture remained rigid, but his gaze darted toward his feet.

"Ha! Gotcha. Idiot." She turned her attention to the liaison waiting ahead of them and tried to pretend the armed guards weren't taking up the rear.

Liz Windsor was cheery as ever as she met them in the doorway where the hangar met the Depot offices. "Welcome back!" She held her arms wide, but it was clearly less an invitation for hugs and more a pantomime for congeniality.

Vel remained sullen, but the grin came easily to Alice. "It's good to be back, Liz Windsor."

The liaison peered past the captain to the rest of the crew, and her smile faltered. "Oh no, did something happen? Your crew looks absolutely dreary!"

"Eh, don't worry about them. They're just tired," Alice explained as Dan shifted anxiously on his feet, checking over his shoulder at the guards. "Shall we come in and chat?"

"Yes! Certainly. A debrief is the next step. But you all look exhausted! How about I get Doug to make you some coffee?"

"Doug?"

"Yes. A new one. Taking Mark's place."

"Wasn't his name Mike?"

"Come, come! I'm sure you have so much to tell me." The crew followed after her tip-tapping kitten heels, and she led them not to a conference room, but the small lounge they'd been in twice before. "Have a seat, please."

Alice and Vel claimed a love seat, Dan slumped into a wing-backed chair, and Caid sat with his legs crossed on the edge of the colorful throw rug that covered most of the cement floors.

Liz Windsor stuck her head out the door. "DOUG! COFFEE!"

She smiled to the waiting room. "It looks like the Depot sent me a buggy version this time. Damaged in the shipping, I believe. Hearing mechanisms aren't what they should be. I do miss Mark's—"

"Mike's."

"—Mike's smooth functioning." She took a seat in a wing-back chair next to Dan's, crossing one leg over the other and clasping her hands together on her knee. She addressed Alice first. "You've told me your decision in regards to our client Aubert Orleans and those he represents. I assume that hasn't changed?" Her arched brows lifted on her wrinkleless forehead.

She was giving them an out. Wasn't this what Alice had hoped for? It usually was.

"No," Alice said. "Our decision—*my* decision hasn't changed."

The liaison pressed her lips into a thin line. "Very well. I've already run it up the chain, but I wanted to make sure you didn't have a change of heart in the meantime. We've smoothed things over with the Yoken people, spoken with Emperor Best himself, and have promised them the necessary gifts in response to the insult. That being said, I must ask: are you *sure* we cannot, in good conscience, match them with any other race?"

The question hung in the air.

Last chance. Alice could erase the darkest fears from the psyches of DeepService Team One with a single word now. All it would cost them was their conscience. The Depot, in its infinite peacemaking power, had smoothed over what

Alice had believed permanently crinkled. Working for a conglomerate like the Depot was a pretty sweet deal. It was nice to have someone on your side, someone with connections.

Maybe it *was* the Alliance who'd stuck that previous DeepService Team One in the cave. Who could say?

Liz Windsor continued to grin at the captain.

Alice looked to Vel, whose expression was stony, though not without a hint of wishful thinking behind those determined eyes. Then she looked to Caid, and he only gazed back with something akin to sadness in his dreamy eyes. Or maybe it was hope? She was terrible at reading holographic emotions.

But it was when she looked at Dan that she made up her mind. Dan, whose prolific fears were arguably his greatest strength, met her stare bravely. He puffed up defiantly, his jaw set despite the pained tightening of his pearlescent skin around his eyes. Then, so subtly that Alice nearly missed it, he nodded.

Alice laughed; she couldn't help herself. Recklessness was fun, if nothing else.

She turned back to Liz Windsor. "The Yoken are absolute nightmares, and I wouldn't wish them on anyone, even themselves, frankly. I appreciate the Depot's efforts to smooth things over, but my answer is the same. No way. Fuck those guys."

Liz Windsor's mood turned somber. "I respect you standing by your decision, Captain Luck. Oh, look! Doug's here with coffee! Please serve yourself." The liaison stood as Doug pushed over a rolling cart with the carafe, cups, and creamer. "I have a call to put into the Depot regarding your final decision. Should be back in a jiffy!"

Doug looked identical to Mike, and Alice suspected that

she could call him Mike and he wouldn't correct her. But now wasn't the time to screw with an android or whatever the hell he was. Instead, she accepted the coffee he handed her. It was the blandest she'd ever had.

Vel placed a hand on Alice's shoulder once Liz Windsor had left the room. "Thank you, Captain."

"I'm proud of you," Caid said. He produced a guitar and began strumming it gently. "You didn't take the easy out."

"What easy out?" Alice asked, trying not to sound bitter. "Saying I'd pair the Yoken with another planet? That's not an easy out, that's a hard … in? No, that doesn't make sense. It's not an out, though."

"It is. And I think you would've seen it as such only a few weeks ago."

Alice took another sip then scowled at the tasteless brew. "I sure hope not." She set the cup down on a side table. "But there might still be a way out of this mess."

"There's no way out," Dan muttered. "We're doomed. I mean, it's okay. We didn't have a good option. We walked right into a trap."

Alice shot him a disappointed scowl. "No way out? Jesus, Dan, aren't you an expert in *weapons*? And isn't there a shitload of them back on *Emergence*? As long as we're that close to firepower, there's *always* a way out." She pointed a sharp finger at the lieutenant. "Don't you start looking at me with those bedroom eyes, Susy, or I'm gonna make you do something about it."

But before anyone had a chance to comment on whether Alice was a genius or an idiot with a death wish, Liz Windsor returned, perky as ever. "I've just spoken with the Depot and relayed your final decision."

The cozy room might as well have been the vacuum of space while the crew waited for Liz Windsor to fill it.

And? thought each of the crew.

"I guess it's time to move on to the next matter of business," Liz Windsor said. "Where would you like to go for your week off? I can begin making accommodations immediat—"

"Hang. On. Just hang on there, Liz Windsor." Alice got to her feet instinctively. "*What?*"

The liaison blinked. "It was stated in the contract. I believe we discussed it as well. Between each mission, the crew is treated to a week off to spend your pay as you wish and recover from the stress of the job."

"You're still paying us?" Dan said. "Like, what, a severance package?"

"Severance?" Liz Windsor chuckled. "Whatever are you talking about, Minister Zone? Why would you need a severance package? You're not resigning, are you?"

"No," Alice said, "none of us are. But we thought ... Well, we aborted the mission without consulting you or the Depot. We botched the assignment, and now you're going to send us on *vacation?* We were expecting a wide variety of responses, but not that."

"Oh, come now, Captain Luck. Why would we have hired you to lead these missions if we didn't trust your judgment? The Depot can't be every place at once, but it serves such an important role in the goings-on of the universe that it *needs* to be everywhere at once. The only way to do that is to hire competent people and trust them. Why do you think we hired you?"

Alice groped for a response. "Because I picked out the right marker color?"

"That was certainly a part of it, yes. But we also trust your judgment, Captain Alice, and if you say there's no hope for the Yoken or the various peoples living on Trauna, then we'll take you at your word. You and your crew have spent the most time with *anyone* from Star Cluster B since the containment barrier went up, so you would know best, wouldn't you?"

Alice blinked and slowly lowered herself back into her seat. "Well, sure. That was our thinking."

"Exactly. You trust yourself and your crew, and we trust you. Therefore, no need to worry about anyone from Star Cluster B ever again. The Depot has taken your recommendation to heart and acted accordingly."

"Acted ... accordingly?" Alice said, looking to Dan for a translation. He frowned and shook his head slightly, but she was starting to recognize his freeze response. It looked like what he looked like just then. "That doesn't sound good. And *which* recommendation did they take to heart exactly?"

"In our last conversation, you said that if any bull or turkey or prize hog acted the way the Yoken had, you wouldn't breed them, you'd take them straight to the slaughterhouse."

"I ... Sure, I said that, but then I'm *pretty* sure I clarified that I wouldn't recommend doing that to Trauna."

"Uh-huh, I remember you saying that. And then you went on to qualify it by saying that if you had to destroy a planet, that would be the one." Liz Windsor's plastic grin turned conspiratorial. "I understand wanting plausible deniability and distance when I hear it, Captain Luck. We read you loud and clear."

"No, but it wasn't ... I didn't ..." Alice's mouth felt dry, and she sipped the bland coffee both desperately and absent-mindedly. "Liz Windsor, tell me the Depot isn't going to destroy Trauna on my recommendation. That's not ... It wouldn't be ..."

"Never you worry, Captain Luck. The Depot has a long

history with these people, and taking Aubert Orleans on as a client was our last attempt to bring the cluster back into the fold of universal peace. Everything you relayed back to us was concerning but ultimately confirmed that there was no hope of rehabilitation. If peace was to be consistently preserved moving forward, they would need to go. Period."

Alice shook her head helplessly. "No. You can't just kill them all. That's ... They'll do it themselves over time anyway, right? Call it off, Liz Windsor. Please. Go back and tell your people not to annihilate an entire star cluster. Tell them I'm forcing you to say it, if you gotta."

Vel rose beside her captain. "Tell them I threatened you."

Dan, too, got to his feet and joined them. "Let them know I still believe diplomatic relations might be possible."

And lastly, Caid set down his guitar and rose. "There's always hope for redemption, Liz Windsor. You know this. You and I have talked about this many, many times. Please, find it in your heart."

"There's not *always* hope for redemption, Mr. Sonorian." But even the grimace Liz Windsor flashed him looked like a grin.

"There is," he said, his voice pleading. "I've seen it so many times. The Yoken are cruel people, but we haven't tried everything yet. In fact, we've tried hardly anything at all. We need to build the universe we want to live in, and the one I want to live in is where people don't give up on each other. Yes, I had to enforce strict boundaries with some of them, but just because they're not ready to change and grow *now* doesn't mean they won't ever be. Please. Call off the Depot. People can change."

"Oh, Caid." Liz Windsor pressed her hands to where her heart would be if she even had one and tilted her head, staring dreamily at the hologram. "That was *quite* a moving speech. You always know how to touch me deeply. And perhaps you're right. Perhaps the Yoken and the rest of those on Trauna could've changed for the better. Unfortunately, the possibility of change ends when a person is dead, which I'm afraid the entire population of Star Cluster B now is. The Depot executed the order immediately. Every bit of intelligent life within the containment field has been wiped out. Fantastic speech, though. I wish I'd recorded it, frankly." She smoothed her hands down her A-line skirt. "Now, who's up for a week of fun in the sun?"

Alice met Vel's eyes, and it was clear enough what the lieutenant was thinking. It was the same thing the captain was thinking, and by the looks of them, the same thing Caid and Dan were thinking.

Shit. We're definitely the bad guys.

PREVIEW: SHIP OUT OF LUCK

PROLOGUE

There was this guy named Betty. She was only a guy in the gender-neutral sense of the word, which most of the multiverse uses without a second thought, because she was technically the egg-bearer of her species. This guy didn't use any of her eggs, though. She kept them for herself and discarded them as she pleased.

She was a wife at one point but had used her six legs, seven arms, and big fucking pincer to escape that nightmare, and now she was one of the revered Lexicographers.

None of them knew this guy was a female. It almost goes without saying that if they'd found out, they would've launched her into a black hole. (There is a strong correlation between having sperm and acting irrationally, but science has never found one-to-one biological causation for this.)

Lucky for Betty, the Lexicographers were a motley bunch, and no two were of the same species. It was rare to find two from the same star system. So, the only way to know the sex of the creature beside you in the Lexicographer symposium cave was to ask, and no one had ever asked Betty. Instead, they had assumed by her name that she was a male, because Betty is usually short for Bettamolllamu, which is obviously masculine.

On this particular day, this guy, Betty, had something important to say. People who've had to hide who they are usually do.

She had called the assembly because, taking up the mantle of her long-dead brethren Dale, Hammy, Garbob, Vince, and Jimjam (not their real names), her pursuit for the name of the guy who was responsible for everything and nothing had finally turned up a fresh result.

Once Betty had settled on the premise that the first two letter of the name truly were HH, she proceeded to formulate the next one in her free time. She found she had a lot of free time now that she was not a wife. Sure, sometimes she had to pack up and move to another part of the galaxy when she sensed a supernova about to explode (old habits of wifery die hard), but she required very little food, as most things with exoskeletons do, and math didn't pay enough for her to own many things, so tidying took all of three minutes a day. That left her with quite a bit of time in her burrow to calculate.

The previous presentations of letters were now legend among the Lexicographers. The first, she'd heard, was presented with a projector on the cave walls, the second in an unnecessary 3D holographic form. If she were to get any respect at all beyond people calling her "this guy," she had to top those.

"Bring in the slaves," she said, scurrying down the steps of the semi-circular auditorium toward center stage.

A side door opened and three naked and chained beings

stumbled through, as if shoved from behind. The onlookers gasped.

Not because of the slavery thing—they were unfortunately cool with that concept—but because of who the slaves were.

Never before had *Homo sapiens* stepped foot upon hallowed Lexicographer ground. The idea was repugnant to most, even in the context of slavery. (*Perhaps especially in that context,* you think. But again, slavery wasn't a big deal to these guys so long as they were not the slaves. However, it's safe to assume they'd start caring if they became slaves.)

"What do you think you're doing?" shouted a halibut-looking motherfucker from the middle of the spectators.

But Betty hadn't engaged her translating software, and since using the common tongue of English to better communicate had long ago been rejected by this group, she had no idea what the fish guy was saying. It had been an intentional choice not to activate her translating software for this. She didn't want to get psyched out. So long as the rest of the group used their tech, though, that's what mattered.

The slaves trudged forward in their shackles, all fleshy shades of brown and shivering. They were taller than most sentient beings, which only served to make their naked bodies appear lanky and awkward as they shuffled toward Betty. She'd already given them their orders ahead of time, and they knew the consequences if they failed to hit their cue.

Keeping their gaze on the floor, they listened attentively, as you can only when your sympathetic nervous system is on high alert, while she began her presentation.

"I have discovered the third letter in the name of that

force that is everywhere and nowhere, the reason your wife left you."

From the crowd: "You smelly turd! How do you even know there *is* a third letter?"

Judging by his tone, Betty felt validated in leaving her translator off. "I have completed the calculations, which you can see here." With a few of her arms, she motioned at the cave wall where, in an homage to Dale and Hammy, she'd projected the formula. "Check it at your leisure, but I assure you that I have not made a mistake. I know the third letter with certainty, and I will spell it out for you with the assistance of the only known survivors of the Star Cluster B annihilation."

"There are no survivors!" shouted the halibut, who really hated Betty for some reason.

"Those are just Homo sapiens from Blerg VFP69," shouted a Lexicographer who was having an affair with the halibut and hoped this verbal support might keep that going.

Betty clapped her beak and ignored the nonsensical hollers it made as the slaves took their cue, shuffled to the center, then lowered themselves flat onto the floor. They wormed their shackled bodies the rest of the way into position, straightening out, their arms straight out above their heads.

"Behold!"

The reaction was delayed, no doubt because math was not usually presented in the form of naked Homo sapiens, but then the understanding shook the cavern.

The three bodies had taken this form:

H

"Horseshit!"

"We already discovered that letter, you cabbage!"

"Do you lack a brain in that head shell of yours? It's the same letter as before!"

Betty figured this would be the initial response.

She rolled her primary eyes. "It's not a redundancy, you void-heads. The name of the force that is everywhere and nowhere starts with HHH. Why is this so hard? You accepted HH, which *no known English word* has ever included, but suddenly, HHH is too much? Get you antennae and eye stems out of your anuses for three seconds."

"It can't be!" came another reply. "It cannot be three aitches!"

While Betty didn't know the specifics of the words being hurled her way, the guy knew incredulity when she heard it. "Sure, fiiiiine," she said. "When three *males* stand up here and tell you there's a double aitch, everyone accepts it. But when a female tells you there are three aitches and even shows her work, you suddenly can't believe it."

"A *what?*" shouted the halibut victoriously. "You're a *female?*"

The chants of *launch, launch, launch* began immediately.

Realizing her mistake, she activated her translating mechanism. "No! I didn't mean that! I don't know why I said it!"

But it was too late.

"Launch! Launch! Launch!"

Betty sidestepped toward the door through which the slaves had entered, but a large invertebrate guard was blocking it, and she was immediately enveloped by the jelly body, unable to escape.

Speaking of the slaves, they stayed right where they were on the ground, but in the chaos lifted their heads enough to make eye contact. What the hell was happening? Was any of this real? One moment they were taking mushrooms at a concert in Vancouver, and the next they were here. What the hell was in those chocolates?

"Don't move," whispered one of them.

"Shouldn't the trip have ended by now?" It had been three days.

"You're just experiencing time differently," said the first, who wasn't entirely wrong. "Don't fight it. The 'shrooms are trying to show you something you need to see."

"The fuck kind of life was I living that I needed to see your balls up close?" barked the connecting line of the H.

"Maybe be a little less worried about genitals, and a little more worried about all this other shit, eh?"

"The point is *not* to worry."

Meanwhile, Betty was dragged from the auditorium, loaded into a pod, and launched on autopilot toward the nearest black hole.

And the Homo sapiens decided to embrace what the psilocybin was telling them—which was nothing because it was long out of their system—and remained on the floor, depicting the third letter in the name of God.

CHAPTER ONE

"Duck!"

Alice Luck did as she was told and was glad she had as the glistening blade sliced through the air right where her neck had been. She shot Dan Zone a wide-eyed look of appreciation.

Stone wreckage spread out around them. Beneath their feet, crushed rock. Around them, what stone pillars remained. Above them, the clear blue sky of the planet Mo'ooz. They'd made it this far, avoided the enemy, and now safety was in sight.

Neither Alice nor Dan had stopped grinning for the last half hour.

"There," Dan said, pointing toward a thick stone pillar farther along on the field of play. "Ample coverage."

Alice locked in on it. Definitely big enough to hide the two of them. "Ready?" she said. "Go!" She feinted like she was making a break for it, then held back, letting Dan dart out ahead of her to draw the sharp projectiles toward him. He blasted three to bits in quick succession before realizing he was without backup, his balls in the wind. Alice cackled from her hiding spot then darted to catch up with him.

Zwarp! Zwarp!

She obliterated two blades in a row, grabbed Dan by the arm, and dragged him the rest of the way with her to cover.

As they dropped down to catch their breath, Dan shivered slightly—a symptom Alice now recognized as quantum jitters. He erupted into maniacal giggles. "Okay, you got me there. I thought you were right behind me."

They high-fived.

This was no hog wrestling, sure, but Blade Blasters was quickly becoming Alice's go-to leisurely activity on their week-long vacation. The adrenaline rush of having multi-armed beings hurl blades at her so sharp they could split a hair in three was unrivaled, and while she'd put Dan's life in legitimate danger by letting him run out ahead of her, *he* had put his life in danger by playing this game in the first place. She liked that about him. The armadillo dude saw the risk in everything … and seemed to enjoy it.

The top of the stone pillar exploded in a shower of pebbles that rained down on their head.

Dan peeked out around the side of their hiding spot. "Almost to the safe zone."

"Great."

"Not great. They've lined up—all of them. They know where we are and where we need to go. It's going to rain blades down on us the second we step out from behind here."

"We have a saying back on Earth, Dan." Alice checked the charge of her blaster. It was running low, but it would be enough; she was built like a linebacker, but sprinted like a wide receiver. *"Don't bring a knife to a gun fight."* She waggled her brows at him, and he laughed.

"I like it," Dan replied. "We have one like that back on Pangoliarch. We say, 'Don't bring a slapper to a blaster bar.'"

"Feels like I'm lacking some context, but I like it. Ready?"

Dan grabbed his backup blaster from his holster. This was definitely a two-handed job.

Alice didn't leave him high and dry at the count this time. Instead, she stepped out first, cackling as the suns' light flashed off the incoming blades.

Zwarp! Zwarp!

"Woop!" she cried.

Zwarp-zwarp-zwarp! Zwarp! Zwarp-zwarp!

"Captain!"

She took her eyes off the incoming blades for a split second and realized Dan was already into the safe zone. Meanwhile, she'd stopped running.

A blade grazed her cheek, and the sting brought her back to her senses. "Balls!" She took off running. *Zwarp-zwarp!*

Dan waited in the safe zone, his arms open as he waved her on. "Almost!"

Three more blades hurled toward her. *Zzzzt.*

Her blaster was dead.

She dodged one just in time and reached for her backup. *Zzzzt.*

Oh right. That *was* her backup.

Ten yards left and no blaster to rely on. She got low.

Something nicked the heel of her Texas-flag cowboy boot, and she cursed. *Not the boots!*

She shot a scowl toward the wall of defenders on the perimeter, but it was short lived. The largest of the armed things was winding up. The curved blade flew, slicing through the air at an angle that made it impossible to judge how severely it would arc.

Zwarp!

It fell from the air, nothing but molten metal now, as Alice made a final leap into the safe zone.

And Dan, who'd left safety to blast away the final threat, followed right on her heels.

She flopped onto her back, panting on the cool green grass at the edge of the playing field, and stared up at the bright blue sky. With each heave of her chest, she let the adrenaline pulse through her veins. The comedown would follow shortly, but for now, she felt indestructible.

Ah, there it was, the dull ache in her arm where a blaster had scorched it on Brittanica. Allura's special cream had worked magic to help it rapidly heal in the last few days, but the heavy use of it on the course was clearly more than a doctor would recommend.

A pearlescent, plated hand appeared in her field of vision, blocking out one of the suns. She grabbed it and let Dan pull her up to her feet.

"Great round, Captain."

"You saved my ass there, Dan. Drinks on me."

"Sounds—wait, you're bleeding."

Alice brought a hand up to her face, touching her cheek.

When she pulled away, her fingertips were red. "Eh, not too bad." Compared to the blaster she'd taken to the arm on the previous mission, this was nothing. The goop Allura had given her for a speedy recovery worked like a charm, anyway. All that was left less than a week later was a small bit of scaring, hardly more than some texture where her skin had singed off.

She poked at her cheek near the wound. "I can hardly feel it."

"That'll change once the adrenaline wears off."

"Then we better get sloshed before that happens." She patted him on the shoulder, but her mirth died when she realized her hand had grazed metal. "What the..." She stepped to the side to get a look at his back. "Christ on a cracker, Dan." One of the blades jutted from his back. "You're hit."

"Huh?" He groped around until he found it. "Oh. Heh. Didn't even notice." He cringed. "Oh void, did it rip my shirt badly?" The blade had lodged itself in Nick Carter's head as he posed with the rest of the Backstreet Boys above a list of tour dates from 1999.

Alice examined it. "Not badly. Poor Nick has seen better days. Maybe not *much* better."

"Nick? Not Kevin?"

"No, Kevin is fine."

Dan found the handle of the blade, and with a grunt pulled it from his armored back, tossing it aside.

In a lot of ways, having a Minister of Weapons and Culture on her crew was hugely reassuring. He could tell her all the faux pas to avoid when they met new species or visited strange planets. He'd undoubtedly saved her ass that way many times already. But she often forgot that he was obsessed with the culture of Blerg VFP69, known to her as Earth or home, and when he dropped strange nuggets like his favorite Backstreet Boy, it made her head hurt a little.

Besides … Kevin?

She'd always been an AJ girl.

"You're alright?" she asked, eyeing the small tear in his T-shirt for any signs of blood. But it was dry enough.

"Of course! I'm fine. Why look like this if the armor doesn't do anything?" He held out his arms demonstratively, and the sunlight danced off the pearly plates poking out of the sleeves of his shirt.

"You're making me feel naked and exposed," she said, then nodded toward lodge—specifically, in her mind, toward the bar.

A few minutes later, as the bartender, who Alice could only describe as "squiggly" took their order, Dan said, "We should probably grab something for Vel while we're here."

"Good call."

And though they ordered a drink for her, Alice suspected the lieutenant wouldn't need it. Vel had taken an immediate liking to one of the beach waiters, and Alice was pretty sure the warrior woman hadn't moved from her shady chair since they'd arrived at the resort five days earlier.

Sure enough, they found Lieutenant Machiavelli right where they'd left her that morning.

"Susy," Alice said, stepping in front of one of the suns and causing Vel to crack open an eye. "Have you even gotten up to go to the bathroom?" She set the cold tropical drink on the small table, next to the fresh one already there.

"Why don't you let me worry about that, Captain?"

"I would, but you don't seem to be capable of worrying about *anything* this week."

Vel shut her eye again. "You say that like it's a bad thing.

Isn't the whole reason the Depot gives us a week off between missions to help us relax and *stop* worrying?"

Alice stuck a fist on her hip. "Technically, yes. But that doesn't mean I thought you could do it."

"What are you saying, Captain? You think I'm overly serious?"

"Yes, that's exactly what I'm saying. And I like that about you, Susy. I need someone to keep us on track, otherwise, it falls to me."

"I would hate to leave some responsibility for you ... Captain."

Alice grunted. "I see the point you're trying to make. Still, *why* are you so relaxed?"

Dan added, "That's what I've been wondering, too. No judgment, just curiosity. Is this how you work through trauma?"

"Trauma? What trauma?" Keeping her eyes closed, Vel reached over and grabbed her drink from the table, slowly and leisurely taking a long sip before setting it back down.

Alice looked around for any possible ghasselite formations but found none. "Were you not on that last mission with us? Did I *hallucinate* you being there when Liz Windsor announced that the Depot had eliminated all life within an entire star cluster because we refused to match the Yoken?"

"I was there."

"Then you know that we're the bad guys."

Though Alice considered it to be the obvious conclusion from the given data points, no one had yet said it aloud, and now that she had, she expected a much stronger reaction than what she was getting from her second-in-command.

Vel shrugged. "Eh, if you want to believe that, sure."

"Of course I don't *want* to believe it," Alice snapped,

wondering how they'd ended up on such a buzzkill of a topic when they *should've* been soothing the adrenaline crash with copious alien alcohols.

"Then don't believe it," Vel said plainly. "You're so great at escaping reality, I'm not sure why you'd stop now that reality is this ugly."

"Because ... because ... someone has to face it!"

Vel chuckled. "Is that what you're doing? Playing Blade Blaster as a way of facing reality? You got a little something, by the way." She gestured at her own cheek, and Alice hurriedly wiped away the blood from the cut, smudging it more than clearing it.

"For the record," Vel continued, "the reason I can relax is because I know what I'm up against now. I understand how this game works. That's all I need to know. Now I can win it."

"Game?" Alice said. "What game?"

"The game we're all trapped in. The one we keep playing." Then, "No, not Blade Blasters. Working for the Depot."

"Please, then, Susy. Explain to me how it works."

Vel took another sip. "No point. You wouldn't listen long enough."

Alice snapped her head toward her lieutenant. "Sorry, what? Crazy bird thing landed in that tree. Go on."

Dan chugged the rest of his drink.

"The Depot is a tyrant," Vel explained. "They will murder large swaths of the universe under the pretense of keeping the peace, but it's really for power. And now I know that as long as we go along with them and occasionally throw them a planet to wipe out, they probably won't kill us. That's how we win."

Alice and Dan shared a bummed look.

"You're okay with that?" Dan asked.

"Of course not. But surviving, given the circumstances, is what I call success. So I'm okay with it. And I'm okay with reading this book on the beach between missions." She held up a copy of *Sucked by the Black Hole*.

Alice read the title. "What … is that?"

"I don't know. Allura recommended it, and you know what? I'm enjoying it. I'm enjoying sitting on this beach, getting drunk in the sun, and reading the dirtiest book I've ever laid eyes on. Do you know how many things I've genuinely enjoyed in my life? Two. This"—she waved the book around, keeping her place in it with her thumb—"and killing my evil twin."

"The fuck?"

Vel waved her off. "It's a long story, but it had to be done. Now, did you need something else from me, or can I get back to reading?"

"Do you know where Caid is?"

Vel pointed out toward the waves.

"Geez, he's still out there?" Alice turned to Dan. "We'd better go check on him."

"I'll meet you out there. I need another." He held up his empty glass.

Alice chugged the rest of hers. "I'll take another, too."

As Dan headed back to the bar, Alice kicked off her boots and shuffled across the sand to the water's edge. As the sea of this strange planet licked at her toes, she shielded her eyes and located the crew's therapist floating on his holographic multicolored raft.

The water didn't get deeper than her waist for a mile out from shore, and though it was crystal clear, she proceeded cautiously. She'd spent too many summers at the Texas gulf coast and had been stung by a jellyfish twice. Those creepy little invertebrates were upsetting enough; she didn't want to think about what shit might exist in the water on a foreign planet.

She called out to him.

He didn't respond.

She called out again, louder this time.

Still no response.

The organic hologram merely continued to sit cross-legged on his raft, staring out into the aqua expanse. He'd been meditating like this for most of the trip, only occasionally checking in on shore to see how everyone was feeling. He seemed uncharacteristically relieved every time they blew him off and he was able to return to this raft in the ocean.

How could someone so ancient be so goddamn sensitive, she wondered.

There was no doubt that he'd been hit the hardest by the unlucky fate of those in Star Cluster B. The whole mission had been upsetting for him, from dealing with Aubert Orleans's moodiness to discovering the bodies of his old crew members in that cave to …

The mass slaughter.

The mass slaughter justified by her decision to terminate the matchmaking mission.

The eugenics mission.

Something sharp and mean stirred inside her brain. A thought. Not a good one.

She blinked it away and realized her eyes were wet in the corners. "Ew." She wiped away the moisture, then put her back to the sea. "Dan!" she waved to get his attention, then hurried over to get started on the next drink.

Continue reading *Ship Out of Luck*: AliceLuck.com

ABOUT H. CLAIRE TAYLOR

H. Claire Taylor is the author of the Jessica Christ comedy series about God's only begotten daughter as well as the Kilhaven Police series about a rookie human cop getting his ass kicked in a city of paranormal beings.

She lives in Austin, Texas, with her husband, John, who laughs at all her dumb jokes and is generally the love of her life.

Claire is also the owner of FFS Media, through which she publishes the books she writes under her four pen names.

instagram.com/claireorwhatevs

amazon.com/author/hclairetaylor

bookbub.com/authors/h-claire-taylor

BOOKS BY H. CLAIRE TAYLOR

The Alice Luck Space Adventures

Lucky Stars (Book 1)

Cluster Luck (Book 2)

Ship Out of Luck (Book 3)

The Jessica Christ Series

The Beginning (Book 1)

And It Was Good (Book 2)

It's a Miracle! (Book 3)

Nu Alpha Omega (Book 4)

It is Risen (Book 5)

In the Details (Book 6)

The End is Her (Book 7)

The Kilhaven Police series

Shift Work (Book 1)

Same Old Shift (Book 2)

Shift Out of Luck (Book 3)

Deep Shift (Book 4)

Wimbledon, Kentucky

See all at www.hclairetaylor.com

Find more books at www.ffs.media